# MARRIED TO A BOSS, SLEEPING WITH A SAVAGE 2

## NIDDA

*This book is dedicated to my muthafuckin dawg City! Right or wrong you have always had my back and I will NEVER FORGET THAT! A lot of people have switched up and switched sides, but you never did! You motivate me to keep going when I feel like giving up. I know that your time away hasn't been easy and you have found out who was real friends and family, but no matter what I will always be here for you! FREE MY MF DAWG!*

# Acknowledgments

First, I would like to thank God for everything! Without him none of this would be possible. I would like to thank my parents for their love and support with everything. My aunt Lisa girl I owe you so much for never giving up on me and continuing to encourage me to keep going! & the rest of my family and friends that have been supportive I love y'all too! Mz Lady P for everything that you have done I will always be grateful!!

To my readers I appreciate every one of you for giving me a chance! More is coming I don't plan on stopping anytime soon! S/O Shay Shay, Janay, keyah, Mari, Tay and Rani! Y'all have all shown so much love! Thank you everybody that has giving me a chance and reading my work. Anybody that has purchased a book or shared the book on social media I definitely appreciate it!

## Keep up with Me

FACEBOOK: NIDDA BIDDA

**Facebook Reading Group: Nidda's Reading Spot**
**Instagram:_Nidda__**
**Thank you again! Don't forget to leave a Review.**

Coming Soon:
_____

A EAST SIDE GANGSTA CHOSE ME 2

**Enforcer and Envii: Down to Ride for a Boss**
**I Found Love in the Dope Man: A Jack Town Hood Affair**

# ONE

## Messiah

_____

Put the fucking knife down and let Mayhem go!" Ivy yelled, from behind me.

*I* heard him cock his gun. Is he going to shoot me? After all that Mayhem did to me and to find out that he was fucking E too. Out of all the bitches he could have been fucking why my wife? Once I found out she was stealing from me we were over. That doesn't mean that shit it's okay for my brother to be fucking her.

"Messiah, you got a few more seconds to drop the knife," Ivy said, now standing in front of me. Mayhem dropped his guns and kicked them away from us. Ivy was pointing his gun in our direction.

"I'm not going to explain to Nita that you killed Mayhem," Ivy said.

Ivy shot his gun right past me and hit the picture on the wall and caused it to crash to the ground. I was weighing out my options fast and thinking of what I would gain by getting rid of Mayhem right now and what I might lose right now if I get it done.

"The way I see this shit, y'all need each other in case y'all forgot. What happened on September 29, 2016, isn't going to disap-

1

pear on it's on. Since that bitch Evelynn is out of the picture; do you want to accept yo part in the situation M? Yea Mayhem was the one that caught all the bodies, but do you remember why?"

I dropped the knife and pushed Mayhem. With my eyes on the gun that was in arm's length of me. As much as I hated to admit that Ivy was right about one thing was that I played my part in the shit as well. Mayhem brought hell to earth that night to save my ass.

~

*September 29, 2016*

*"Messiah, can we just go out for a little while?" Lay asked.*

*She already knows that I hate the fucking club. I need to take my ass home in the first place. She just wants the next bitch to be able to see her with me. For what I don't know because I'll never leave E and we've already that conversation.*

*"Alright, get dressed. When I say it's time to go its fucking time to go or yo ass will be left at the fucking club," I said as I got out the bed to jump in the shower, so I can get dressed.*

*I called Mayhem and he didn't answer. So, I called Killa, to see what club they were going to tonight. Every Friday and Saturday night Mayhem is in the club, he doesn't miss a fucking weekend. The club ain't never really been my thing. I can drink at the house and bitches are everywhere. I got the info to the spot where they were going to be at tonight and went back to getting to get dressed. I'm not spending my night in a club with her and her thot ass friends and none of they broke ass niggas trying to get put on.*

*I got out the shower and got dressed Lay walked into the room wearing a black tight dress that fit her ass tight. Lay is bad as fuck and always has been. Caramel complexion, tall, long, jet black hair, and covered in tattoos. She can get on my nerves; with expecting too much already knowing my situation at home. We ain't even left yet and I'm already ready to be back.*

*I made my way out to my truck and Lay is right behind me. What she doesn't know is that if Killa and Mayhem weren't out tonight we wouldn't be going either. Bitches can never just be satisfied with what you give them they just always want some more. We made our way to the club.*

*Lay lives downtown so, it didn't take long for us to get there. I found a* parking spot and we made our way in. As we made our way to the long ass line, I saw my man's C at the door. If this bitch doesn't make her way behind me her ass will be outside waiting in this line. I reached into my pocket grabbing a rubber band and shaking up with C. He removed the rope and let me in not checking me. Telling the other nigga at the door that leads to the club "I already got him!"

I see Killa, Mayhem and some bitches across the room in VIP, so I grabbed Lay hand and we made our way over there. "What the fuck are you doing here with her?" Mayhem screamed over the music. I just looked at his ass; the same thing he is doing with this bitch Ray-Ray. I went back to check out the scene you never know who the fuck is going to be in the club. Lay grabbed a bottle off the table and took it to the head and Mayhem was about to cuss her ass out. Killa started killing himself laughing. I motioned my hand for Mayhem to chill tonight because I don't plan on being here too long.

"Get up! Get up damn you that drunk that you can't fucking hear!" Mayhem screamed, pushing Ray-Ray off him causing her to spill liquor all over me.

"Damn! Nigga you just made her spill that shit all on me!" I screamed.

Mayhem was out the booth making his way across the room, knocking niggas and bitches over in the process. I took off my jacket that is covered in Belaire and handed it to Lay because I knew some shit was about to pop off with fucking Mayhem and this is exactly why I don't come out.

"If I'm not back in five minutes, go get my fucking truck and be parked in the back in the alley," I said handing Lay my keys.

Killa and I made our way over to where the commotion was because I know that's where the fuck Mayhem is. My brother is a real nigga and one thing for sure I know that he always has my back! That is why I always have to be there for him even when he is always on some good bullshit. He had a nigga on the ground by the bar, stomping him the fuck out. Three niggas where making their way through the crowd and they were ready to get Mayhem off they nigga.

I pulled out my nine and Killa did the same. Them niggas started busting but didn't hit shit. All they did was make a bunch of bitches scream and get the fuck out the way. Killa and I laid both of them niggas down and Mayhem put a bullet in the nigga's head who was already near death's door.

We made our way out the back Lay was right where her ass was supposed to be. She jumped in the passenger seat and Killa and Mayhem jumped in the back and I got us the fuck out the parking lot. As I made my way to the highway, "Damn nigga you just left that bitch Ray-Ray at the club," Killa said over Jay-Z that is bumping through my speakers.

"Fuck that bitch, she acts like she didn't hear me say get the fuck up; that nigga almost got away!" Mayhem said, in between hitting his blunt.

"You are going to stay the night, right?" Lay asked.

I acted like I didn't hear her. Evelynn, thinks I'm out of town for the weekend so I can without having any issues when I get home. Lay started off as fun something to get me away from the shit at home. At times I feel like E don't understand the shit I go through in the streets for us to live this life. Between having to deal with Mayhem shit and then on top of that the pressure and the necessity to keep shit right and everything moving smoothly can be a lot at fucking times.

When I'm at home I should be able to relax and have some fucking peace. That hasn't been the situation lately. All I hear is I want this and buy me that. Shit, I am happy to leave town or to make my way over to Lay's when I can. Lay is rubbing my dick through my jeans as I pulled up to the spot where Killa and Mayhem were going. I handed Killa my gun, so he could get rid of it.

"I'll get with you in the morning, so we can handle that," Killa said as he got out.

"Alright Bra, we should do this again, without that hoe up there doe!" Mayhem, said slurring his words trying to get his self together as he got out my truck.

I pulled off and Lay was unbuckling my jeans and my shit is already hard as a rock. Lay wasted no time taking all my down her throat. I was trying to focus on the road and get back to Lay's as quick as I fucking can. All you can hear is Jeezy coming through my speakers and Lay slurping. I finally made it to Lay's and pulled into the driveway. She wasn't stopping anytime soon and shit I didn't want her too. I'm pushing my dick as deep as it can go down her throat and she still ain't stopping.

"Fuck, Lay," I managed to spit out.

As I came Lay swallowed all that shit up, not leaving nothing. Just like I knew she would she had my shit back ready and jumped right on it. I let my seat back as she did her thing. I let her be in control as long as I could. I started to beat the fuck out of her pussy from the bottom. She was getting tired, I could tell by the way she was breathing and starting to slow up.

"I loveeeee yooooou Muuurda!" Lay screamed out.

I didn't answer I just kept on doing what I was here to do. Lay was biting my neck holding on to me for dear life. "I hope it's good nigga! Cuz, it's about to be a fucking drought where you are going if you don't do exactly what the fuck I say!" A nigga screamed as he snatched open the driver side door. Lay jumped off me and the other doors flew open. I'm wishing I would have kept my fucking gun for tonight. The nigga at the driver side had a gun to my head and the other niggas had their guns all pointed towards me.

I leaned down to pull up my pants. If these niggas wanted to kill me I would have been dead these niggas want money. That's what the fuck everybody wants. The little money that I have on me and my fucking watch; I can't believe this bitch been plotting to set me up doe. After all the shit that I've done for this bitch; it's my fault for getting too damn comfortable with her ass. The only people that know where I am at is Killa and Mayhem.

"Nigga get the fuck out the truck!" I don't have all fucking night! The nigga with the gun pointed to my head screamed.

I'll be damn if I beg or scream this is the life that I chose to live, and this just happens to be something that can happen when you fuck up and get caught slipping. As I followed behind one of the niggas the other still had his gun pressed to my head. As I stepped over the threshold, I was hit in the back of my head with the gun and all four of the niggas began to stomp me. After a few minutes, they stopped after the nigga running the show felt that I had had enough. Two of the niggas lifted me by my arms and pulled me from the ground; while another nigga ran my pockets.

"Get yo brother on the phone!" The nigga with the gun still pointed at me said, handing me my phone.

I dialed Mayhem's number while plotting to get the fuck out of here and my ass home still breathing. Fuck it I'm about to go for all that I fucking know to survive. These niggas are getting sick of holding me, so they are loosening their grip. The nigga to my right barely holding me anymore. I hit the nigga on my left with my right and his bitch ass fell to his knees. The other nigga tried to grab me from behind, just like the bitch he is. I headbutted his ass; he's going to have a fucking headache that he'll never forget. Soon as I turned around to run, the nigga had his fucking chrome to my head.

"Nooooo! Ray, don't or we won't get the money!" Lay screamed.

"When I get my money; maybe you'll make it home. Maybe you won't. My

5

*bitch pussy is good ain't it! That mouth is even better huh?" Ray said, attempting to taunt me.*

*One thing I know for sure is that Mayhem will kill this nigga whole family if I'm not let the fuck out of this house. I fucked up; I always make moves thinking about what the fuck could happen or go wrong but in an attempt to get away from my fucked-up situation at home. I fucked up and didn't thoroughly think what dealing with this bitch could bring to me. I had a smirk on my face, so this nigga knows how I'm laying and being worried is the last thing on my mind. He better be fucking worried. He didn't like that, so he hit me across my face with his gun, I stumbled, but I didn't fall so he was hot.*

*This nigga is a fucking pussy; he not going to shoot me. All I got is my fucking hands and this nigga about to feel them; I charged his ass and he dropped the gun and it flew across the hardwood floors. I dropped the nigga to the ground and started to beat the fuck out of him. The two bitch ass niggas pulled me off, Ray. Ray got up off the ground, leaning against the wall. "Get y'all shit together. Tie this nigga up before I kill one of y'all!" Ray screamed. The bitches took heed to their orders. Lay handed one of the niggas some rope and started to tie me to the chair.*

*I still was looking at the nigga with the same smirk. He was already mad, but I can feel the heat coming off him now. My phone started to ring, and Ray grabbed it off the table. "Muthafucka you got my money?" I could hear Mayhem going the fuck off like only he could. A nigga that is about to make a come up; should be smiling and ready to fuck up some commas. I know my brother so, I know he is talking some shit.*

*"Nigga talk all that boss talk; see if yo brother makes it out of here breathing!" Ray said and put my phone down on the end table.*

*"What the fuck y'all waiting for! Go get my fucking money!" Ray screamed the two bitches, that had tied me up, made their way out the house.*

*It was just Lay, Ray and this other weak ass nigga left. Being in this type of situation fucks me up mentally. I can't think straight. This is a time when I need to think and come up with some shit quick and fast.*

~

"I wish you would shoot one of my muthafucking son's muthafucka! Nita yelled as she came busting into the room.

Rossi came in right behind Nita with two of his men, and picked up Evelynn, "I'll be in touch." Rossi said on his way out.

"Dijah, get Killa to a doctor! Steel get the fuck out of here and Chaos, back to fucking work!" Nita screamed at the top of her lungs.

"Where is Harmony?" I asked.

"Did you care why y'all up here trying to fucking kill each other!"

"The only reason, I'm letting you slide calling me a muthafucka is because of all this, I wish you would ever think about it again," Ivy said, picking up on the chairs that we flipped over.

Dijah, Steel, and Chaos got Killa out the room. I looked over at Mayhem while trying to decide if I would be able to ever forgive my brother. Would our relationship ever be the same again? He was my first friend, the nigga I caught my first body with, and now as I look this nigga I hate him more than anybody. This nigga is a momma's boy, he not going to kill me in front of momma.

"Muthafucka, muthafucka, muthafucka! You can leave any time now! Maurice and Messiah sit the fuck down!" Nita screamed.

"I'm not going no fucking where dear until this shit is resolved," Ivy said sitting next to Mayhem across the table from Nita and me. All the blood all over Mayhem's face and clothes l can only imagine what the fuck I look like.

"Neither one y'all don't have anything to say?" Nita screamed.

"Damn momma could you stop screaming," Mayhem said.

"No, I can't, so this whole time y'all have been trying to kill each other?"

Mayhem looked everywhere but Nita. I made sure the guns I had under the table were still there who knows where this conversation is going.

"So, Maurice who shot you at the club?" Momma asked.

"I did," I said.

"Nita, let me talk to you for a second", Ivy said getting up from the table.

Nita didn't say anything smart which surprised me she just got up and they left the room. Mayhem and I just stared at each other. My phone started vibrating in my pocket, it's Chaos.

"What's up?"

"They not sure if Killa is going to make it M."

"Alright, I'll be up there in a minute."

"Arie doesn't want you up here."

"What the fuck you mean she doesn't want me up there. What the fuck does Arie have to do with Killa?"

"She been fucking him," Mayhem said staring me in the face.

"Alright, stay up there I'll be up there."

"That's why you shot Killa?"

"Yup," Mayhem said.

Ivy walked back into the room. Nita wasn't with him. He's always in the middle of Mayhem and me, and I know he's sick of it. Mayhem is reckless and doesn't give a fuck about anybody but his damn self. I was willing to just go our separate ways but that wasn't good enough for him.

"I don't have all day, so I suggest y'all get to talking," Ivy said as he sat down at the head of the table.

"Mayhem you're wrong and you made shit the way it is. Messiah, you married the wrong bitch," Ivy said.

I didn't need anybody to tell me that I married the wrong woman. Ever since this shit that has been going on between E and me, I haven't been able to stop thinking about that my damn self. When I first met, E I was in a relationship with Alicia and I broke her heart by getting with Evelynn. Every chance that Ivy gets he brings that up. I haven't seen Alicia in years, but my family will never forget about her.

# Mayhem

As I looked at Ivy and Messiah, I know that with them I can get what I need. As mad as I am with M, I'm madder at Killa and Arie. I did make everything the way it is, and I don't give a fuck and I stopped caring a long time ago. I wasn't trying to make Evelynn my bitch, and M knows me well enough to know that. Ivy knows what it was even though we never discussed it. My phone started vibrating its Trina.

"What?" I screamed into the phone.

"Don't what me! What is so important that is preventing you from seeing Miracle? What the fuck makes you think we're getting a divorce? What do you want me to tell Rossi?"

"I don't give a fuck what you tell Rossi, bitch we've been done! You know that we've been done in case you forgot! You might want to remember who the fuck I am before you call me talking crazy again," I spat and hung up on her.

I'll deal with that later. Nothing is going to change. My business with Rossi is done. I don't owe him anything and he owes me nothing. Unless it has something to do with Miracle, I don't have shit to say to Trina. Nothing is different. As far as Arie, I wouldn't spit on that bitch if she was on fire fuck her.

"So, what do you want us to do Ivy, hug, and makeup and go back to how shit used to be? It will never be same again."

"So y'all both out the game because yo dumb ass got niggas robbing pharmacies and what are you doing are you going to be a citizen?" Ivy asked.

"This nigga getting shit from Miller, yea I know I'm fucking his wife too that's what I do I go the club and ask bitches are they married and if they are they can get a night," I said.

I could see the sweat coming down M's face he was mad as fuck and even madder that Ivy is in here and Nita is in the house. At this point, I'm just going to listen to what M has to say. Ivy is right about one thing I'm on my dick and at this point, I need a lifeline to be able to keep my shit! Ivy was just shaking his head. M was just looking at me like he wanted to come across the table and I wanted him to so bad.

"So, what do you want to do?" I asked.

Shit, I know the part I played the night that I saved my brother. M has always thought he was the smartest nigga. This night he fucked up, he was with some bitch and she set his ass up for some niggas to rob him. They got everything M had and still wouldn't let him go so I had to bring them, niggas out which meant I had to do what the fuck I had to do.

∾

*September 9th, 2016*

*"None, of your niggas can't go sleep until my brother is back out here! Take y'all asses to seven eleven and get a fucking five-hour energy muthafuckas!" I screamed.*

*Killa came through the door "Where the fuck does that bitch live?" Killa asked. I don't fuckin know where she lives, or I would have just gone to the fucking door! I rubbed my hands over my face, "What the fuck you niggas waiting for! Get to the fucking block find out where that bitch lives! Her fucking momma, grandma and anybody that share the same blood as that bitch!" I screamed, Rico, Black, Blu, and Smoothe made their way out the door.*

*I went behind them. Once I got on the open porch, "find out who she fucks* with and where their people sleep too all them muthafuckas bout to die tonight!" I screamed and went back in the trap and slammed the door behind me. Killa was on the phone trying to get some information. I can't help, but to pace around this muthafucka! I never liked that bitch and I tried to tell Messiah not to trust that bitch. Look what the fuck is going on now! All because of a bitch; that didn't mean shit to this nigga and now we are paying out money that could have went to something fucking else!

"That bitch Lay fuck with this nigga Ray, and his sister stays around the corner," Killa said snatching his keys off the coffee table and making his way to the door.

I grabbed my gun off the shelf and made my way out too. I jumped in the car with Killa and he skirted away from the curb as hot as I am shit, I could have run around the damn corner. Killa didn't bother stopping at the stop sign and pulled up on the fucking curb. I jumped out and ran up to the door and kicked that muthafucka down. I don't have all night. If I don't get the fuck home before the sun comes up, Arie ass will be out here looking for me.

"That's that nigga fucking sister," Killa said grabbing the nigga that was sitting on the couch up by the collar of his shirt.

"Where the fuck does Lay live?" I screamed walking up to the bitch, my gun leading the way.

"I don't know. My brother doesn't bring her around us. He has a wife, please just let me go," The bitch managed to say between crying hysterically.

"Call yo fucking brother right now!" I said, helping myself to the bottle of Hennessy that was sitting on the end table.

The bitch jumped up and grabbed her phone and made her way over to where her phone was plugged up to on a charger. She is still fucking crying, "Bitch, shut that crying shit the fuck up! Before I give yo ass something to cry about!" I screamed, taking the bottle to the head again.

"Nigga, this ain't time for no fucking drink break," Killa said while letting off a round into this bitch's nigga leg.

"He isn't answering, please just let us go. My kids are here," The bitch said in between her still fucking crying!

"Didn't I tell you to shut the fuck up?" I screamed losing my patience.

I finished off they little ass bottle and made my way over to her crying ass. I put two bullets in her head and one into her pussy. The nigga Killa had on the *ground is now holding his leg, he's crying harder from the bullet the fact that I just sent his bitch to crossroads.*

*"What's yo bitch password? Nigga don't waste my fucking time you look like the type of nigga to read yo bitch text messages!" I said, between laughing.*

*This nigga just got that pressed nigga look his face; the type of nigga that will take a bitch phone and hold it waiting for the next nigga to call. "2322," The Nigga screamed out.*

*"Get the message out, I'm not playing that nigga better call this phone in thirty minutes or I'm coming back to get you and going to let you watch me kill yo fucking momma!" I said, on my way out the door.*

*Killa was right, behind me. I opened the passenger side door and turned around and went back in the house. "Do yo fucking job and you don't have to watch yo momma die, but I'm still coming back to kill you," I said and left back out.*

*"You didn't kill that nigga, did you? How the fuck is he going to deliver the message dead nigga?" Killa said before I could close the car door.*

*"Naw, I didn't kill him nigga relax! I had another message for him," I said laughing and lighting my blunt.*

*My phone started ringing it's this nigga Rico he better has some good news, or his ass can go too. "That nigga that Lay fuck with wife live on Albion Street, I'll shoot you the address to the other phone. I'm outside the house." Rico said.*

*"What the fuck you are waiting for get yo ass in the fucking house before you buried next to them muthafuckas!" I screamed and hung up.*

*Not only do I have to make sure that niggas eat, I got to stand around and hold they are fucking hand for them to know that it's time to work. My burner started ringing, it was the address to where the house is; I told Killa and we made our way to that bitch. I kept checking the bitch I just took care of phone to see if anybody had called. Still no fucking call; the longer I wait the more muthafuckas going die! I need to be fucking driving; this nigga being too cautious driving to damn slow for me! When we get to the house, I'm kicking Rico out of his shit and fucking driving myself.*

*My phone started ringing I looked down and it's my momma. "Yea, momma what's up?" She started screaming in my ear asking where M was. When momma gets started, it takes her a minute to calm down. When shit is going down, even if don't nobody tell her it seems like she always knows. "Momma calm down, I'm handling it!" I attempted to scream over her loud ass.*

"Raise, yo muthafucking voice at me again the niggas in the streets will be the last of yo fucking concern muthafucka!" Nita screamed.

"Momma as soon as I handle this shit, I will come over there," I said, and she hung up in my face.

We finally made it to the spot with this Morgan Freeman driving ass nigga. I jumped out the car and Killa and I made our way into the house. Finally, these niggas take some fucking initiative they got the niggas wife tied up. "I don't have much time, so where does yo niggas bitch live?" I asked the woman ripping the tape off that was covering her mouth.

"I don't know what you are talking about I haven't seen Ray in days," The woman cried.

I don't believe that she doesn't know where her nigga bitches stay. What type of woman is she? I checked Ray's sister phone and it started ringing. "Where the fuck is you dropping my brother off at?" I asked, as soon as the phone connected.

"Nigga what did you do to my sister!" Ray screamed into the phone.

"I would take some of that base out yo voice homie cuz I'm about to do the same thing to yo wife and everybody that's breathing,"

"Nigga, do you know who you fucking with? Ray asked.

I couldn't help but laugh as I walked around the living room. Looking at this nigga pictures of his family. Looking at this cheap ass Rent-A-Center furniture; I'm starting to get the message of who the fuck this nigga is.

"A broke ass nigga, that can't afford Ashley's or fuck nigga American Furniture Warehouse," I said laughing.

That nigga was hot, he hung up his fault because now his wife has to go too. "I'm going to give you one more chance. Do you know where yo nigga bitch stay?" I asked, losing my patience.

"No, I don't know anything about no bitch," The woman pleaded.

"Maybe you'll do better next lifetime, kill this bitch!" I said and made my way out the front door.

Killa made his way out and he was on the phone. "Nigga one of them nigga homeboys, stay up the street. Come on, so we can get this shit over with," Killa said. I'm not riding with this nigga. How long does it take to shoot somebody got damn! As I looked at the house these muthafuckas finally made their way out.

"Naw, I'm driving what's the address?"

Killa gave me the address and jumped in his car and made his way up the street. "Give me yo fucking key!" I screamed, and Rico threw his keys to me.

*These niggas must know now that I don't have any more fucking time to play they got they ass in the car. I smashed, up the street, not giving a fuck no more. A lady that must have been out trying to get some fucking exercise I hit that bitch and kept going. I already know that I'm going to have to argue with Arie in the morning because I don't see myself going home no time soon.*

～

"The way I'm looking at it. People work with people they don't like every day. You don't step on my toes and I'll do the same. Play yo role and I'll continue to play mine. You don't shoot at me, I —"

# Messiah

My phone started ringing it was Rossi. I didn't think we had anything else to discuss, but I answered anyway. Mayhem didn't have shit else to do today.

"Yea," I said.

"I don't know how but Evelynn isn't dead and I'm just guessing you didn't know but she's pregnant. You have a son, I just—"

"What the fuck do you mean she's pregnant?"

"My driver is pulling up to get you," Rossi said and disconnected the call.

I took a deep breath and rubbed my hands across my face. How the fuck didn't I know that she was pregnant? I don't put anything past Evelynn, the money and shit could be replaced. Not telling me about this, I don't know how the fuck I feel.

"How long have you been fucking Evelynn?" I asked.

"Right after I killed the paralegal bitch."

"Where the fuck are you going?" Ivy asked as I stood up to get in the shower, so I could leave.

"Evelynn isn't dead and she was pregnant, with my son."

～

As I walked through one of Rossi's home; following behind one of his men I still don't know what to think or how to feel. All types of emotions began to come over me. Once we got to the room where the baby was inside of an incubator with tubes and machines hooked up to him. Rossi came into the room with a doctor. I didn't give a fuck about Evelynn or how she was doing I just needed to know what is going on with my son and anything else didn't matter.

The doctor explained to me that the baby suffered from apnea. He discussed with me the complications and explained to me that he would do whatever he could do to ensure that my son survived. I just kept looking back at my son, if the bitch would have told me she was pregnant I would have handled things differently. I can't take it back I just have to do whatever needs to be done to make sure that Harmony and Messiah Jr are okay. If that means I have to work with Mayhem for a little while longer than so be it.

"So, Mr. Jones as far as your wife goes—"

"I don't have a wife, anything that has to do with her I suggest you talk to him," I said, turning to walk away and went to see my son.

# Arie

Chaos was looking at me like I was the scum of the earth. I don't give a fuck about what nobody thinks about me and my actions it was okay for me to stay with Mayhem for years with him fucking other bitches but as soon as I decide I'm done, I'm wrong. I'm waiting for Krystal, Killa's sister to get up here to the hospital. With my shop being fucking destroyed this is the last thing that I need in my life right now. Killa's mom doesn't want M here but I don't know why. Killa and M have been friends forever and I know that he will do whatever needs to be done to get the nigga that did this to him.

As I lift my head, from getting my drink out of the vending machine I saw somebody I never thought I would see again. I thought our past was buried and he was given so much time he would never see the light of day. Steel is still the finest man that I ever laid eyes on his smooth chocolate skin is smooth and his body looked even better than I remembered. Looking at him and his fresh cut just made my pussy began to throb after and leak like only Steel could make it.

"Wassup Arie?" Steel said.

"Hey."

I had to get the fuck out of this hospital. I damn near ran into two nurses and a little kid trying to get to the elevator. I'll come back later. Once I made it to the elevator. I pushed the button repeatedly like it was going to make it come faster. When I was with Loon, I was also seeing Steel. At the time I knew that it was wrong because he was with Khadijah, but nobody knew about it what we had but me and him. When I felt somebody grab me I knew it was Steel. His touch, scent, and presence just took me back. It started off as an escape from my reality turned into something that was much more for me, but I can't say the same for him.

Back in the day, this man could call in the middle of the night and I was coming. I made up so many aunts and uncles who ended up in the hospital in the middle of the night just to get out the house and can get to Steel. I would stay out at night until the sun came up and fight with Loon all day. By the time, I started fucking with Steel, Loon and I had been damaged beyond repair.

"Damn, that's how you feel. Try to run out the damn hospital," Steel said.

I didn't know what to say. We both made our way onto the elevator. When I got with Mayhem, Steel ran across my mind, but since nobody ever knew about us it didn't matter. I wasn't going to let it stop me from being with Mayhem. My heart is beating so fast I thought it was going to jump out of my chest and clearly Steel could feel it as he took me into his arms. The way that he held me in his arms, I had forgotten for a few seconds where the fuck I was at. I tried to pull away, but Steel kept holding me.

I never thought I would see him again. As far as I was concerned he was something from my past that never happened and that's the story I have been going with and plan on continuing to go with that lie. I pulled away from Steel and made my way off the elevator once it made it to my floor.

I knew that Steel was following me to my car and with each step I took, all the memories of me and Steel started to consume my mind. As I went to pull the handle to get into my car, Steel wrapped his arms around my waist and removed my hair from my neck and kissed my neck, while putting one of his hands down my pants and touching my drenched box. I lost my breath and turned around and wrapped my arms around Steel's neck before I knew it. I felt so safe and secure whenever I was in Steel's presence I never had any worries because he was there. He wasn't one that a muthafucka would try and even though he when we were together he was mine and that's all that mattered. I love Mayhem, but I'm addicted to Steel. Like a crackhead can't leave the pipe alone I don't know how to leave him alone.

Steel removed his hand from my pants and loosened his grip on me. His fingers that were drenched in my juices he sucked them one by one. I didn't give a fuck who was in the parking lot and if anybody may have noticed what was going on between us. The feeling that I got right now is a feeling that no other man has yet to give me.

"Did you miss me?"

"Yes," I replied before he could even finish his question.

I wrote a lot of letters to Steel while he was away, but I never sent any of them. I just drank to try to forget about him, but it never seemed to fully go away. I wrapped my arms around Steel's neck and he kissed me with so much passion. As or tongues intertwined I had a feeling that I can't explain. Anything that Steel wanted from me he could get and even though I tried to suppress those feelings they're still here. Steel was unbuckling my belt while I was unbuckling his and pulling his jeans down. Steel ripped my panties off me and started to rub the tip of his dick against my other set of lips.

I was gasping and moaning, and he hadn't even put it in yet. As I bit Steels lip he eased long, thick and perfect dick into me I bit Steels neck. He lifted me off the ground and fucked me like it was going to be the last time. As I threw it right back like I would only do for him. I closed my eyes and took it all in. I never thought that I would see Steel again and be able to hug, kiss, touch and be able to feel him ever again. This is so wrong, but it feels so right. For him to be here right now none of my problems mattered.

～

As Steel and I sat in Denver's Biscuit Company and as he reached across the table for my hands. As he looked into my eyes, I felt like something was on his mind. If he wanted me to know he would tell me, so I let it go. After we reunited in the parking garage at the hospital, he wanted to come here. My phone started ringing it was Krystal, I just let it keep ringing until it went to voicemail.

"So, you're with Mayhem now?"

"No," I said snatching my hand away.

I knew this would be something that would eventually have to be discussed but I wasn't expecting that would need to be right now. If he had an issue with me being with Mayhem while he was away, then he should have addressed before he played in my pussy. Mayhem and I are done and I'm not going back to him. The only reason why I will communicate with Mayhem is because of B and nothing else.

"It doesn't matter to me. No matter what you will always be mine. Even with the time that has past, how I feel hasn't changed," Steel said as the waitress came to table with our food.

The hold that this man has had on me for all these years is crazy and the way that I would normally act with anybody else I couldn't bring myself to try that shit with Steel. Steel was gone for seven long years.

"You and I were something, that was between us. Mayhem and I were in a relationship and y'all relationship has nothing to do with me."

When I met Mayhem, I was a single mother struggling trying to build up my clientele working in somebody else's shop and make a better life for B and I. Mayhem started off as just my friend and after some time we became more than friends. A part of me wishes that Mayhem was dead, but for B's sake, I wouldn't want to have to explain that he will never see Mayhem again. I would be lying if I said that I still don't have any love for Mayhem, fucking with Killa didn't just make those feelings go away.

I caught Steel up on everything that had been going recently. I can't run down the last seven years during breakfast. As I sat talking to Steel and eating it was like he had never left, and we just picked up where we left off. I'm moving into my new home in two days and I'm happy to not have to worry about Mayhem being able to come and go as he pleases. We will be meeting at public places for him to get B.

"I'm getting a divorce Arie."

"What?"

I never thought that I would hear those words come from him and it was never something that I ever asked him to do. I never thought that he would leave Khadijah and I let that go a long time ago. He explained to me that things hadn't been right between the two of them in years. Before Steel went away we never discussed his marriage and anytime he attempted to say anything I just cut him off. I didn't want to hear about her; I avoided that topic at all costs. I heard everything that Steel was saying, and I didn't know how I felt about it. My phone started ringing again. I needed to get back to the hospital before its time for me to get Brandon

# TWO

## Arie

---

*I*t's been a month and Killa is still on life support. Messiah comes up to the hospital every day to check on Killa and everyday Killa's mom Joanie causes a scene. That hasn't stopped Messiah from coming. Messiah and I have never had a problem before. I know that he and Mayhem have had issues but that never had anything to do with me. Messiah won't speak to me or even acknowledge me anymore.

At this point I don't give a fuck I'm not trying to come to no Sunday dinners and I don't care how anybody in their family feels about me I could care less. Steel and Messiah are across the room by Killa whispering but I have no idea what they're saying. My phone started ringing so I made my way out the room to answer.

"Hello," I said.

The caller didn't say anything. I walked out the room and said hello again assuming because of me being in the hospital my reception is bad, still nothing. So, I hung up. I've been getting calls like that for about a week from different numbers. I don't know who the fuck it could be and the last thing I need is to be dealing with some bitches playing on my phone right now. I know it's a bitch because

23

only bitches play on phones. I made my way back into Killa's room, Messiah made his way out.

"Are you okay?"

"What the fuck did I do to M?"

"I don't know."

Steel and I were back like we never skipped a beat. My only issue with Steel is being around him at the hospital with Killa being in his condition. Not only was I fucking this man's brother but his homeboy too. Krystal wants to keep Killa on life support, but his mom wants to take him off.

In the short amount of time that I had been seeing Killa, we had become very close. One minute he's saying he's going to M's and the next I'm getting a call saying that he's been shot. Killa's baby momma has been calling worrying Krystal not about Killa's status but her financial rewards if he doesn't make it.

"I got to shoot this move, I'll meet you at the house later," Steel said in between kissing me and Making his way out the room.

I'm waiting for Krystal to get here so I can go and get B from my mom. I want Killa to wake up and can here for his son. I know how much Killa cares about his son and no kid should have to grow up without their father.

My phone started vibrating and it was a text from my mom. Wait until I tell you what yo favorite cousin did now. I knew she was trying to be funny but was talking about my cousin Leesha. It's always something with this bitch so I can only imagine what she did now. She is a few years older than me, but she just can't seem to get her life together no matter what. I don't know what it's going to take. She has two grown kids but decided a few years ago to have another baby. I'm sure she did just leave her daughter with one of my sick and elderly aunts again and then decided to go missing.

The hospital phone started ringing which was strange who the fuck would be calling his room. I got up to answer the phone.

"Hello."

"Is he fucking dead yet?" Destiney, Lil Killa's mom screamed in my ear.

"No, you stupid dumb bitch...," I attempted to say before she hung up.

I've never had contact with Destiney, but I knew who she is from back in the day. The way Killa lives wasn't anywhere close to Messiah and Mayhem So I'm sure he doesn't have a will, life insurance or anything else. Steel told me Messiah was going to his house before one of his family members did but if he didn't I'm sure Destiney did or is going to. I just want to know what the fuck does she want or expect to get if he does die.

Somebody knocked on the door. I looked up and it's Krystal. I caught her up on what I knew from the doctors, but nothing has changed and the way their family is feeling they could take Killa off life support any day now.

# Trina

---

I couldn't get my dad involved in my business with Maurice and that is the only thing that I thought would secure my position with him. Without Maurice being my husband there is no way that I will be chosen to take over the family business. Even with all that is going on within the family with Evelynn, Rossi made it clear that he will be meeting with me and my cousin Candy in two days. I have to go back to Colorado because my dad has to be there for a while for business.

"Mom, can I call my dad?" Miracle screamed as she ran into the living room.

I picked up my I Pad and called Maurice for Miracle. I don't facetime him, so if he's not busy he'll answer for her. I know that he is not able to come here because of him trying to recover but this divorce shit caught me by surprise. I need to get to Colorado to find out what's going on between Arie and Maurice. I don't give a fuck what they do but no bitch is going to come in between me and my place on the throne.

Maurice and Miracle were talking and hearing his voice right now just only make me more furious than I already am. I was born into this lifestyle and I was raised being told that I needed a man that could run shit and could financially provide for me. When I met Mayhem, he was that and more. I had never met anyone like him before. When I first moved to California my father was against it, but he allowed me to go if one of his bodyguards were close by. I learned how to lose them fast, so they never prevented me from getting the full California experience.

A part of me was hurt when Mayhem decided that he didn't want to be with me anymore, but I also wasn't ready to settle down. I wanted to live my life and not have to answer to anyone. We decided it would be best for us to get married to keep the peace between Rossi and Mayhem. Mayhem still provides for me financially and that was all I wanted at first. With Mayhem coming to California so much once Miracle was born the feelings I had started to come back but I know that was only because I couldn't have him because he was with Arie. I've always known about Arie, Mayhem is so damn honest that it hurts at times.

He doesn't give a fuck what he says or how it may make you feel. I made my way upstairs to finish packing our bags. Mayhem has no choice, but to continue to be my husband I don't give a fuck if he got three girlfriends, a bitch, and a hoe. We must remain legally married if I want to be able to take over.

～

"What do you mean I can't take over without Mayhem?" I asked Rossi.

I knew exactly what he meant, and this is what I was worried about. Evelynn can't do anything she can barely walk. My ghetto ass cousin Candy and her husband are being considered. Rossi is ready to step down and Mayhem and Messiah no longer want to do business with Rossi.

"You can't do this alone, you're not ready," Rossi said, and Moretti co-signed. I took a shot of Hennessy to the head. I'm going to have to try to talk to Mayhem and get him to understand what this could mean for our future. Or maybe I'll start with that bitch Arie.

I got up to storm out the room I could hear my uncle Moretti talking shit as I walked out the room. He just wants Candy to take over because he wasn't there for her as a kid. O fucking well she can get the fuck over it.

I damn near ran out the house and jumped into my rental to go to Aries' shop.

❧

I watched Arie as she talked to some white man and the police. I had been sitting in the parking lot watching her for a while. I already know that Mayhem did this. He really cares about Arie; in a way that he never has or will for me. I pushed my feelings to the side and reminded myself what the fuck is at stake right now.

My phone started ringing and then Mayhem's name flashed across the dashboard. I noticed Arie was going to the car, so I sent Mayhem to voicemail, so I could see where his bitch was going.

As I followed Arie I got even more furious. This bitch couldn't just play the role I was allowing her to have she just had to fuck it up. Things had been going just fine for years. Some bitches just will never be satisfied.

As Arie pulled up to a house a man came to her car to greet her. It wasn't Mayhem. I was trying to see his face and then he turned in my direction making eye contact and it's Sharief. The way he was rubbing and kissing all over Arie was damn sure not like brothers treat their brother's bitches for sure.

He must have told Arie to go in the house and then he made his way in my direction. I know that Mayhem is crazy, but I know what to expect from him because I know him but Sharief is a whole different type of nigga and with the look in his eyes I'm going to have to get rid of him and his brother if I can't get Mayhem to see things my way.

# Steel

I got enough shit to worry about then to be arguing with Khadijah right now. I gave her the opportunity to be on my side and shit she chooses Messiah and the rest of them muthafuckas over me. My hands were tied I didn't have any more options left. The amount of time they were going to give me I couldn't do. The first case was seven; that I was willing to do without a problem. Once I got locked up all these other cases that they had against me started to pile up. First, they wanted Mayhem, shit I figured he would have hung himself by the time I got done with the time I had, but that didn't happen. Then they wanted me to give them Messiah too. I explained to Khadijah what I was doing for her and the kids from the beginning she was against it. Once she made that decision she was against me and we must go our separate ways. After this shit is done and over with I'm going away and I'm never coming back.

"Look, Khadijah, it ain't no going back what's done is done. Those muthafuckas don't give a fuck about me. They worried about them!"

The kids my sixteen-year-old daughter Sharieffa is at Cheerleading practice and my baby boy Lil' Sharief is in his room, I know he can fucking hear us. I'm sick of arguing about the same shit over and over. Now Khadijah all of the sudden doesn't have anything to say. Fuck it, I got up and grabbed up my phone that was ringing so I can get back to handling my business. I never had to question whether Khadijah was down with me or not. She always been down to ride from the beginning. For her to turn her back on me now that is some shit that I don't think that I'll ever get over.

Khadijah didn't follow behind or beg me to stay it was like she was willing to let me just walk away and never come back. Fuck me! I don't love Arie, I never have to, but I know that if I ever called her she was coming. It was easy, and I didn't have to do any extra. For years it worked for us and since she done with Mayhem we back where we left off. Once I made it to my car and got in, I looked up at the house thinking about all of the years Khadijah and I have spent together and now it's over.

～

"Look bitch, what I'm not about to do is play with yo dumb ass. I'm none of Mayhem and I don't give a fuck about yo daddy or none of yo uncles bitch!" I said as I thumped Trina in her face.

I'm already having a bad day and this bitch thinks that whatever she wants she gets. She already knows who she is fucking with. So why she picked today to try me I don't know.

"Okay, I don't care what you and the bit..." Trina attempted to say before of smacked her to the ground.

Arie ain't my wife or my woman and depending on how she takes how I'm living she probably never will be, but this expensive hoe not about to call her out her name. My phone started vibrating it was Messiah. I sent him to the voicemail.

"I'm sorry, I need help and I'll pay you any amount of money I need this shit done. So, I can get my spot."

I was looking at the dumb bitch waiting for her to say what she needed but she didn't say anything. She just looked at me and the more she looked at me the more furious I got. I got some patience but dealing with dumb disobedient bitches isn't something that I do.

I refuse to even hold a conversation with a dumb bitch. I walked away from Trina trying to not put my hands on her again.

"Bitch what the fuck do you want 1, 2," I said pulling out my gun and cocking it.

She and every other muthafucka in these streets know when I get to three I'm shooting ain't shit else to discuss.

"Okay, okay look I need Mayhem dead."

I wasn't expecting that Arie ain't no fucking Killa I don't know why she is damn near stalking her. I thought about it and weighed out my options. Once I testify I'm disappearing, but the state wants Mayhem bad him coming up dead is going to cause some shit but as long as they get Messiah. That should more than enough. They got to go it's either them or me, while I was gone they were all out here living their life so.

"I want twenty-five million and I need it by midnight tomorrow. Get the fuck out," I said opening the door and walking to the back of the house.

That bitch damn near ran out the house, if she knows like I know she'll come up with the money because either way she got to die too. No loose ends I can't take any chances. The bitch ain't my baby momma.

# Messiah

That was the quietest plane ride I've ever been on in my life. Mayhem and I have got to meet with Lady Heroin and I'm just ready to get shit back all the way right. Finding out that Evelynn had hidden the fact that she was pregnant from me is something that is still hard for me to accept but getting shit back on track in the streets is something that I got to do because I now have two people that are depending on me.

As Mayhem and I stood outside the airport waiting for Lady H's driver to get there it was an awkward silence which made it uneasy for me. If the nigga was talking shit, I would at least have an idea of where his head was at. We've been around each other a few other times but we say the bare minimum and keep it moving. I need to know that when we on the same page when dealing with Lady H.

I know that she wants some shit handled before we can do business which is understandable, but Mayhem needs to understand that we have to do shit the right way because one fuck up and it could cost us everything that we have. My phone started vibrating it was Rossi.

"Yea."

"Evelynn is awake," Rossi said.

"You know I don't care."

I'm trying to figure out how he goes from wanting her to die to now he has an entire nursing staff nursing her back to health. As soon as I get back home I'm moving Messiah jr out of Rossi's. Everything is set up so that he can be properly taken care of. He's not coming to the house yet and Harmony is still with Nita, but they'll be going to a safe house until I figure some shit out. I know that I'm going to have to argue with Nita to get her to leave her house. At this point, she doesn't have a choice. I listened to Rossi while texting Preston to file the motion for our divorce. I ended the call with Rossi I need to be focused and Evelynn is the least of my worries right now. He could do whatever the fuck needed to be done with Evelynn.

"Do you know what she wants us to do?" Mayhem asked.

"Naw."

Who knows with her. It could be something simple or some extravagant shit. Right now, I need what she can get us. Miller shit ain't working and even though I don't agree with a lot of Lady H's practices she can get the job done. Lady H's driver pulled up the curb and Mayhem and I looked at each other. We both knew what we were getting into with dealing with Lady H, but Rossi is out of the question.

We both knew what we are in the game for. I have children that I have to be able to provide for and I could have gone a different route, but this is the life I chose. If I'm a drug dealer I'm going to be the best damn one that anybody has ever seen.

As we rode to Gasparilla Island to Lady H's I looked out the window at the water that surrounded us. I needed to make this shit work because after I handle a few things I'm out the game. I know that Mayhem has every intention to stay in the game until the day he's laid to rest but this ain't no forever shit to me. The only way that Mayhem and I will be able to do business is if I just let him do his own thing and that's what I plan on doing.

~

As we rode on Lady Heroin's yacht I just wanted to get this over with, so I could get back to my kids.

"You Alright?" Mayhem asked.

"Yea, I'm cool."

"Sorry about the wait I had to handle some other things. Let's get down to business I'll deliver whatever you want to anywhere you want just to give me two streets that cross anywhere in the world the package will be delivered. I just need one thing from the both of you." Lady Heroin said as she made her way up to the upper deck.

"What you need?"

"I need you both to pick up something for me. Y'all ready?"

"Yes," Mayhem and I both said at the same time.

She gave us instructions about what she needed to be done. If Mayhem and I never agree on anything else the money is something, we'll always agree on. I powered on the prepaid I'm using for the next few days to let Chaos and Dijah know it's coming. Chaos responded right away. Something is going on with Dijah, I made a mental note to check on her when I get back. She has been off lately, I don't know if something is going in her with her and Steel, but she's been late doing everything I've asked her to do. All it takes is one time being late and make a mistake and everything we've fought for will be gone in the blink of an eye.

I can feel Mayhem looking at me as I turned to look at the water. Whatever I need to do to get closer to retirement is going to need to be done. So, if I got to work with the devil for a little while longer than so be it. Mayhem is plotting to do some extra shit I already know. I just don't know what the fuck it is yet.

"Y'all personal issues aren't going to interfere with this deal is it?" Lady H asked.

"Naw, we got this," Mayhem said.

Lady H's two henchmen carried in a man by his arms that is beat the fuck up, one eye is swollen shut and the other is hanging from the socket up to where we were standing.

"Y'all don't recognize who this is?" Lady Heroin asked.

Mayhem and I both looked at each other. I had never seen this nigga before in my life. Mayhem said he didn't know him either.

"Yea y'all know him it's Smoothe."

I looked a little closer and it is Smoothe. What the fuck could he have done to Lady H? He's never met her, and I've never even mentioned her to him.

"Since Ivy reached out to me about talking to y'all, I had my people checking out a few things. I don't know if y'all know but Smoothe got picked up a few weeks ago."

All the shit that has happened over the past few weeks I didn't know that Smoothe had been picked up why the fuck wouldn't he had told me that?

"He's one of the feds star witnesses on the case they attempting to build against y'all", Lady Heroin said.

I would never have imagined any shit like that after all that we have been through. Looking at Smoothe got me questioning a lot. I know one thing for sure and two for certain Mayhem will kill me before he tells on me. As Lady H people held Smoothe up from smacking the deck. Before they dropped him Mayhem and I riddled his body with bullets. I needed to find out what the fuck he had told them, but he wouldn't be able to testify where he was going.

Lady H's men disappeared and came back with rope and blocks of cement. Mayhem handled the upper body and I handled the lower. We got him tied up and threw his ass overboard once Lady Heroin gave the go. I need to get to Preston to see what the fuck is going on but first, we had to deal with Lady H's requests. Having to fuck with Mayhem to clean up the shit that I started is still something that I don't know is a good idea, but what fucking choice do I have.

～

*September 9th, 2016*

*As I sat looking at this nigga Ray I'm just waiting for him to untie me. His niggas finally made it back with my money. This little money ain't gone last long; they don't know what to do with it. Ray is pacing around the living room floor; shaking and shit. I can't take this nigga serious he just doesn't have any idea of what the fuck he is doing. He didn't make any plan and he has no idea* what he's about to do next. Everybody knows that my brother doesn't have it all so he about to cause hell and this nigga whole family about to feel it.

He had shattered my phone a while ago; the fact that my shit was ringing and he ain't had a call the whole time we been in this fucking house I'm sure is what got too him.

"Muthafucka if you touched my wife; I'm going to kill yo whole fucking family!" Ray screamed into the phone. Mayhem said, something to this nigga that got him even madder than he been all night.

"Nigga, I'm coming to see you!" Ray screamed.

This nigga ain't ready for how my niggas coming, he can't even take control of a fucking ransom. He gets face to face with Mayhem and his nine and he is going to freeze up. I've seen it happen before. Some niggas want to be a boss so bad, but when they get in the position to run shit they don't know how to. That's the type of nigga he is I'm sure. Ray paced the floor a few more times. This nigga can't even afford the latest shoes; his Jordan's is running over, and he is wearing a cheap ass dingy t-shirt. I knew these niggas was some broke niggas when they took my damn Gucci loafers off my feet and this nigga that's supposed to be muscle has my fucking jacket on, that's covered in Belaire.

"Watch this nigga! If he breathes too hard handle that shit!" Ray screamed as he made his way out the door with Lay on his heels.

Before that nigga Ray made it around the corner two of the niggas made their way out the door. I know these niggas are broke so, I offered what the fuck made this nigga heartbeat. I watched how he was moving, this nigga on his phone not even paying no attention to me. This nigga is young and green I can smell that shit; he doesn't even want to be here he just wants the money.

"I can put you where you want to be. You not going to get but a pinch out that fucking bag and you know that. I can get you to the fucking table so that you can eat. You'll never have to worry about yo child support payments or none of that shit. You'll be able to give yo baby momma and yo whole family enough money so that you won't have any problems anymore," I lied more money more muthafucking problems.

This nigga was all ears and started to tell me about all his problem like I'm a fucking therapist. I fed him some more bullshit; I got to get the fuck out of here. I have a wife and family that I have to get home to.

# THREE

## Messiah

$\mathcal{J}$'m up shit lately I haven't been able to sleep a lot. Other than Chaos I don't know who the fuck I can trust. Khadijah has been on some other shit, she not focused I don't know what the fuck is going on with her, but I got to go holla at her in a minute. Steel trying to stay as clean as possible, but I know when he gets off papers he'll be reliable. I got to get this shit under control so that I can get Harmony and Lil' M and get the fuck out of here. Mayhem and I are trying to work together. It's hard to work with somebody that you don't know if you can trust. Hasn't been any bullshit between us lately but who knows how fucking long that's going to last.

Knock, Knock, knock.

Who the fuck could be knocking on my door? I grabbed my gun off the nightstand and made my way downstairs. The closer I got to the door the louder the knocks got it's the fucking police.

"What the fuck do y'all want and why are banging on my damn door?"

"We have a warrant for Evelynn Jones arrest," One of the officers said while the others pushed past me and made their way into my home.

The officer handed me the warrant. I looked over to see what this dumb bitch has done now. Murder? This bitch couldn't have murdered anybody. What reason would she have to murder anybody? I called Preston, so he could get the fuck out here, so I could get over to Rossi's and see what the fuck is going on. As they ran through my house destroying shit like they do, they decided that they hadn't found anything and made their way out.

"Were going to get her," an officer said.

"Good, please do."

Preston was busy so he's not able to meet with me now, so I got to go check on my kids and then go holla at Khadijah. As I made my way to see my kids I started to think more and more about making changes to be done with this shit. This shit will worry you to death. Between dealing with niggas in the streets and my own damn family I don't want to do this shit forever. I'm ready to be done and live a simple life and raise my kids.

~

As I turned into Khadijah's drive mile long driveway; I could see the police lights and hear the sirens going off. I went a little further and I could see them running through their home like they had just done mine. "Fuck!" I screamed while hitting the steering wheel. Now I got to deal with more bullshit. I called Preston again, he going to have to find some fucking time to deal with this shit.

"Look, Preston, the police are at Khadijah—"

"I Know, I'm here. Get the fuck away from here. I'll meet you at the hideout, in an hour," Preston said and hung up.

My phone started ringing and I'm not in the mood for no more bad news. Against my better judgment, I answered.

"M, Killa is gone," I heard Krystal, but I couldn't believe it. My nigga, my best friend is gone and at the hands of my brother.

I hear Krystal talking but everything after Killa is gone I didn't hear. Shit, it didn't matter to me what difference does it make? I finished up talking to Krystal and promised her I would be to see her in the morning. As I sat outside the hideout, my mind just seems to be going a mile a minute. Somebody pulled up behind me in the driveway, once they killed the lights I saw it was Mayhem; so, I got out the car.

"What the fuck is going on right now?" Mayhem said.

"Nigga yo guess is as good as mines."

"I got some more fucked up news, Evelynn is up."

As we made our way into the house I found where Nita was she was sitting in the room watching Lil' M where she usually sits. She wasn't going to like what I was about to tell her, but they got to get the fuck out of here as soon as I can get the doctor to clear it. The only person that needs to know where they're at is me. I just watched Lil M and Nita from the doorway, I'll talk to her later. As I made my way into the kitchen Mayhem's drunk ass was already drinking. Drinking is not going to change any off this shit right now. Honestly, I need this nigga to be sober and his head in the right place because who knows what the fuck is about to happen.

"Hi, Mr. Jones are you hungry? Would you like me to get you anything?" Guadalupe asked.

"No, I'm good Guadalupe. Thank you."

I'm waiting to hear from Chaos. He has been running shit in the streets. He knows how to handle his own, so I don't have to worry about him. The niggas that he got working under him they move like he says move and if he catches any funny shit he won't hesitate to set shit off, so he's about the only thing right now that I'm not worried about.

Nita walked into the kitchen and I wasn't ready to talk to her yet. She just wanted to be nosy any damn way to see what is going on. Just when she was about to start with her questions Preston was at the door. I could hear Mayhem telling her everything he knew; it's enough going on to have to hear her damn mouth right now. The look on Preston's face told me that shit was about to get worse. Khadijah has never had any issues and never been arrested. The police were running through her house like they do mine.

"Look, somebody is talking, but I don't know who. Khadijah is looking at a lot of time. Whoever it is knows a lot. Is there anybody that you to know that could have switched sides?" Preston said while laying out thick manila folder filled with paperwork.

Mayhem and I looked at each other. I can say a lot of shit about Mayhem, but he would never tell. We weren't raised that way. The only people that know shit that could hurt any of us would be Nita, Ivy, Dijah, Steel, and Chaos.

"Nobody that knows anything important wouldn't be talking to nobody outside," Mayhem said.

I looked up at Preston and just when I thought shit couldn't get any worse it did. "This is coming down soon, I don't have a date yet."

It's an indictment for Mayhem and me. I handed it over to Mayhem and Nita snatched it out of his hands. I looked down at my phone it was Steel. I answered to make sure that he and the kids are good.

"Wassup," I said.

"I'm good dealing with this shit with Khadijah. She is not getting a bond."

"Preston is on his way down to check on her, you and the kids good?"

"Yea we straight."

I ensured Steel that I was going to make sure that Preston did everything to get Khadijah home. He told me, he and the kids were good. I got to deal with Killa's people and hopefully, Mayhem just agrees to keep his distance because anything else will just cause more issues than anything.

"I'll be in touch, I'm going to check on Khadijah," Preston said.

Mayhem walked Preston out and Nita was standing in front of me wanting to know what Steel was saying. After I finished talking to Steel I handed Nita the phone she snatched it out of my hand, I went to check on Harmony and Lil M before it's time for me to go. The nurse Allison was in the room checking on Lil' M.

"When do you think that it will be okay for Lil'M to be able to travel?" I asked.

It's going to be a few months, he's not ready now. Let me go get the doctor for you," Allison said.

That's not going to work; I need to get them the fuck out of here way before a few months from now. These muthafuckas don't know everything and he could start progressing. If he's anything like me then it's going to take a lot to keep him down and stop him. As bad as I want to walk away from this shit; right now, that ain't an option that I have.

∿

*September 9th, 2016*

*This nigga who now I know his name is Bic is getting comfortable and he dumb as hell. So, I know I got him where I want him to be. "So, look, all that money in the bag is your for start but as soon as I can get out of here," I spit out. Shit, I don't have all morning, shit the sun bout to come up in a minute. Bic is thinking, he is fidgeting with his hands and them muthafuckas itching. I already know how this shit goes. He started to untie me just like I knew he was.*

*"Nigga, I'm ready to get this money. Whatever you need I got you; just let me know," Bic said. I didn't waste my time responding.*

*He got me untied, "Let me see yo phone," I said. He handed it to me. I called Chaos; let him know where I was at, so he could come and get me. He on his way, I tried to call Mayhem, but he didn't answer. Bic went down the hallway. I looked around the room for his gun that I remember him laying down. I picked it up and made my way down the hallway. He was coming out of the bathroom, "Where you need me to take you to?" Bic asked.*

*I shot him in between both of his eyes. He wasn't taking me do damn where, but I sent him to where he was going. I heard the front door opening. I made my way back down the hall and gave both niggas the same shit that they nigga just got. I could hear Chaos, car booming, so I made my way outside with my fucking money.*

*"Damn nigga, what the fuck is going on?" Chaos asked.*

*"Nigga I'll tell you when we get to Nita's."*

# Evelynn

"What do you mean you can't tell me where my baby is!" I screamed at the Nurse.

"Mam, you really need to lie back down, I will go and get Rossi for you Kirsten said and made her way out of the room.

Trina came into the room and just was looking at me like I'm fucking freak the mighty. I know I looked crazy. I made the nurse cover up all the mirrors in the room because I didn't want to have to look at myself. I hope that Messiah is dead, and I can get myself together and get Harmony and go on with my life.

"Rossi will be in to talk to you in a few," the nurse said standing in the doorway and made her way down the hall.

I'm not going to be able to stay here long. I appreciate everything that Rossi has done but this isn't going to work for me. I need to get out of here. Everyone is making me feel uncomfortable from the nurses to Rossi jr He keeps walking past the room and the look that he gives me I have never had anybody give me before.

The hate that he has for me, I will never understand. I don't want anything from Rossi and have never asked, but with me being in my current condition I'm going to take everything that I can until I can get to Messiah's money. I know that I am going to have to fight

Nita for it, but I'm his wife we were never divorced so everything is mine. Rossi made his way into the room and Trina didn't move. This bitch can get the fuck out, I barely know her. My business is my business and she doesn't need to know anything about what I have going on.

"Are you okay? Rossi asked.

"Yes, I'm okay. I just want my son."

"You will not be able to ever see your son or Harmony again,"

"What the fuck do you mean I'll never be able to see them again—"

I attempted to say before something was placed over my head and I was hit in my head harder than I have ever been hit before. I was trying to catch my breath and I began to start gasping for air. All the wrong I have done none of that involved Rossi. How can my father sit and watch someone do his to me and Harmony ran across my mind until everything faded to black.

～

I'm not sure how long, I was out. I was already in pain from the bullets that had riddled my body but the pain that I'm in now is like no pain that I have ever felt before in my life. I blinked my eyes attempting to concentrate so that I could see what is going on around me. I was able to concentrate on an older woman that is sitting across from me. I turned to look for Rossi and or Trina and the pain the shot through my body is indescribable as I screamed out in pain I was met with a warm hand across my face.

"Shut the fuck up," I looked up and it was Rossi jr,

"Can you get the nurse, I need something fast," I pleaded.

"No more nurses bitch! Welcome to hell on earth."

The woman sitting across from me started to walk towards me. She had something in her hand, but I wasn't sure what it was until she got in front of and I realized that this bitch had a chainsaw in her hand. I have never been religious, and I don't pray much, as I think of all the wrong I have done I don't know if God is even listening to me anymore, but all I can do is pray that he is. Rossi appeared and kissed me on the forehead and back away. I started to beg and plea with him to please not do this to me and to please just give me another chance. My cries and pleas fell on deaf ears and Rossi moved out of the way.

"I started to kill your mother when she betrayed me, but I got way more satisfaction making her suffer every day. Knowing that she is suffering makes my days better. So, I decided that it was the time that you get to know your mother for the rest of your life," Rossi said.

"Don't move!" The woman yelled.

"No, please, please don't do this to me."

One swift motion my right hand was taken off, by my mother while my brother and father watched, like this shit is normal. The pain that I am feeling is hell, I wish that Messiah would have killed me. What type of people would assist me in getting me better; just to inflict more pain on me.

# FOUR

## Mayhem

---

*A*s I hugged and kissed Joanie on the cheek, I could feel someone starring a hole through me. I figured it was Messiah, but it was Arie. I flicked the bitch off and walked over to the casket to lay my rose on top of it. I made my over to where Messiah, Ivy, and Steel were standing. Even though nobody knew but us that I was the one that killed Killa. I still needed to be secure and I can tell by the way that Messiah looks at me that I can't depend on him. We are both dealing with each other because we have to at this point. As soon as we get some of this shit taken care of were done with each other for good.

"How is Khadijah doing?" Messiah asked.

"She good, she ready to stand tall," Steel said.

Khadijah wasn't somebody that we had to worry about talking to the feds, but it's somebody that we need to be worried about. Messiah and I both agreed, it was time to clean house and hit the block ourselves and make sure that we are good from all angles. Failure to do so will have all of us gone forever and a day. Before Messiah and I handle some shit, I have to go check on Miracle and try not to kill Trina.

"He's all yawl's, figure it out!" Destiny Screamed loud enough for everybody in the funeral home to hear, pushing Lil Killa in our direction.

Destiney turned to walk away, and Messiah and Krystal were on her heels. I know that Messiah is going to take on the responsibility of taking care of Lil' Killa because that's just the type of nigga that he is. Destiny is about to get fucked up doe. She has been acting crazy for the past few days, so I'm not surprised that she did this shit today. She has been demanding money, dope or jewelry and I'm not sure who the fuck she think going to give her ass anything. Ivy and Lil' Killa walked away going to view Killa for the final time before they close the casket.

"Y'all need me to do anything?" Steel asked.

"Naw, not right now. You just got home, chill for a min," I said.

"I can't chill. All the time that Khadijah facing I need to be able to get back to it."

He was right, but I know that Messiah, is taking care of Preston I'll let him handle one thing and go from there. Arie walked over to where Steel and I were standing. I needed to make time for B real soon because I haven't seen him in a minute but looking at this bitch had me ready to set it the fuck off at this funeral home.

"Are you going to handle Preston this week and make time for B?" Arie said as she walked up, and Steel walked away.

"Yo nigga didn't tell you where his stash was at before I killed him?" I whispered in her ear, bit it her ear lope and made my way to handle my business.

I'll have Nita get B because the next words I say to Arie will probably be before I kill her. Unless I decide to just let her live; we'll see how I feel. On my list of things to do, she isn't at the top but she definitely working her way up there as I knock this other shit down.

❧

"I'm not about to argue with you Trina get over it! I'm not going to be with you ever again! Miracle come here!"

I'm getting her away from this bitch, she doesn't care. This bitch is refusing to sign the divorce papers, but she is going to sign them before I leave this house. She is making this way more difficult than it has to be. Nothing will change about our previous arrangement. I don't give a fuck about her daddy or none of the fucking family but I'm sure that's what she so damn concerned about.

"Miracle, get your jacket and go to the car with Paw- Paw," I said.

Trina's eyes got big, but she knew better than to get crazy with me in front of Miracle. Looking at me crazy is all this bitch better do if she knows what's best for her. As Miracle made her way out the door, I pulled out a copy of the papers that I needed Trina to sign to get this shit over with.

"Sign right there and hurry the fuck up, I got other shit to do!"

"Mayhem no, I'm not we can figure something else out."

It isn't shit that we could figure out and this bitch was going to learn today. I grabbed Trina by her neck and rammed her into the mirror hanging on the wall, in her father's condo she's staying in while she's in town. The mirror shattered, and pieces flew every-where. Every time Trina screamed out from the pain the more I knocked her head on each wall in the room. If she could have stayed in her place a lot of shit that's going on in my life wouldn't be an issue for me. I figured Trina had enough, so I grabbed her left hand forcing a pen into it.

"Bitch get to signing it!" I said as I kicked her in her back and walked away from her, to check my phone that is beeping in my coat. It was Steel texting me, I got her. We're in the warehouse.

Trina threw the pin and got up off the floor. She had signed the papers and that was all the fuck that mattered to me. She'll get over it and be back to fucking and sucking by morning. I made my way down to my car and my phone is going off again. It's fucking Steel. Why the fuck is this nigga blowing up my fucking phone? Here niggas go acting like bitches; this is some shit that I don't have time for. This nigga ain't no fucking rookie, one thing I don't have time for is holding no grown man hand! Khadijah got to get from under these charges.

Not only do I have hold Steel's hand. I also have to make sure that M is doing what the fuck he needs to do. I know that M knows how to ride but is ready because shit is about to get thick. The last time this nigga wasn't thinking is the reason we in most of this bull-shit now.

~

*September 9ᵗʰ, 2016*

*I done killed too many fucking people to count tonight and still ain't no fucking closer to getting to Ray or finding out where the fuck M is at. As I sit in front of this last house and check my rearview mirror; I see Killa coming down the street finally. I put them, other niggas out. This ain't a fucking shadow night to learn how to be a gangsta. They have been getting on my fucking nerves all night. I got a fucking headache. I don't know what the fuck Chaos could be calling me for, so I sent his ass to the voice mail.*

*I shot as I made my way up the stairs to the house. Somebody is screaming, but I won't be happy until some more muthafuckas are dead. I kicked in the front door and one nigga's head is damn near blown off. Two other niggas are balled up in the corner crying harder than the bitch that's screaming bloody murder. I sent hot lead through her ass; these niggas know the most. Killa snatched the big nigga off the floor and stood him up on his feet.*

*"Where the fuck does Lay stay at?"*

*"Man, I don't know wher—" The nigga said before I killed his ass.*

*The other nigga could see his death coming too, so he ran off where Lay and her whole damn family lives. Little does he know I don't give a fuck about shit and he still got to go! Killa put two bullets in his head and we made our way out the door. I ran to car and Killa was behind me smashing down the street. My brother better be fucking okay or Lay's family is next. That bitch family needs to go anyways, just because.*

*We finally made it to Lay's and the front door is wide open. What the fuck is going on? Ain't no fucking way this nigga is up in there. I still got out, Killa was already at the door going into the house. Just like I figured as we ran from room to room. The only people that are in this muthafucka are two dead niggas. My phone started ringing and I check it it's Nita again.*

*"Momma, I'm still looking for him," I said.*

*"Nigga this is me come to Nita's, M said and hung up.*

54

# Khadijah

---

It's too late, I should have told Messiah What Steel was doing way before now. Preston is working on my case and is down here pulling me out of my cell damn near every few hours. Nothing he can do is going to change any of this. Steel knows everything there is to know about me. Everything that I have done he can run it down and I'm sure he has. When I visited him a few years ago and he told me that he was going to turning fed and wanted me too as well. I thought he had lost his mind. I had to play it cool because I know making the wrong move he'd kill me. Telling Messiah and Mayhem would have had me dead before the words left my mouth.

I'm loyal to the soil and even for my husband, the man I would have put before anybody; I'll never change that. Preston is trying to find out about the secret witness, but I know it's Steel. If the feds are still working on their case, they're not going to let that shit out until they have all the information that they need to be able to bring down the entire family.

"Khadijah, do you have any idea who could be against you?" Preston asked for the hundredth time.

"No."

Telling Preston would be just like telling Messiah and before I lay my head on my bunk tonight, I'll be dead. I'm just going to do my time and accept the fact that I married a snitch. Preston was talking, but I wasn't listening. I needed to call my sister Samaya and make sure that she doesn't let Steel take my kids. If Steel gets my kids I'll never see them again.

"Preston, I need you to make sure that M, gets money to my Samaya for my kids. Whatever is going to happen is going to happen. I'm ready; I have to deal with it."

"I'm going to find out who it is that's talking and make sure that he doesn't make it to testify," Preston said leaning over the table and still whispering.

I made my way to the phone to call my sister. Each step I took, I felt like I was going down in the quick sand. The only thing that I regret is not being able to be there for my kids. I know what it's like not to have either one of your parents around. As much as I convinced myself time and time again the sacrifices that I was making in the streets was to ensure them a better life. I never imagined that their father would consider doing the opposite. I was waiting for the call to connect and going to try to be as civilized as possible while talking to my sister. Samaya and I have had a strained relationship all of our lives.

Samaya is the exact opposite of me. She was the good girl that stayed away from the streets and married a white man that was her ticket out the hood. As much shit, as she talked about my lifestyle, it didn't stop her from asking for money every chance she got when her knight and shining armor left her ass for Becky with the good hair a few years back. My dope money was good enough to keep her from going back to the hood then.

"Hello, are my kids okay?"

"Yes, they are fine when exactly will I be getting the money?"

"It will be to you by tomorrow morning. I need you to make sure that Steel does not get my kids Samaya."

"I'm not going to let Steel get the kids, I promise."

I heard what she was saying, but I need M, to get that money to her right the fuck now. Money makes that bitch world go around. Until she has the money in her hands or in a designer bag is when I will be able to halfway sleep. As I talked to my kids, I thought about other relatives that may be more suitable but as much as I despise Samaya she is the only option I got. The rest of my bloodline is way worse than her. I don't know how I'm going to explain to my kids that I am never coming home. The only way that they will be able to ever see or hug me again will be in a prison visiting room; filled with other families.

The day I must, it's going to break my heart but looking my kids in the eyes and explaining to them that their father is the reason for the season we are getting ready to go into is going to be even harder. I never imagined that this would be my life. A girl walked by the phone and handed me a piece of paper. It read you still have time to come to the winning team. Your loyalty should be with me your husband.

I wiped the tear that was falling from my eye. This entire time I have kept them from falling and I can't let them fall not now. My strength and my faith are all that I have now to be able to get me through this situation. Samaya told me she would bring the kids to see me. I need to see them and tell them what's going on, waiting isn't going to do any of us any good.

# Messiah

---

"Momma, I know that you are not going to like this, but I need you to take the kids and go out of town," I said.

"Why? What the fuck is going on?"

"Nita, it's hot as fuck and to be honest it's not about to get better right away. I need to know that you, my kids, and Lil' Killa are safe."

Momma didn't say anything, I know she is mad, but she'll get over it. Right now, I need to make sure that they are okay, and nobody can get to them. I'm the only one that needs to know where they are at and I'll get to them as soon as I can get everything under control here. My phone started ringing and I was relieved because I could feel Nita was getting ready to start tripping and now, is not the time for that.

"Yea, Preston what's up?"

"I need you to get to Samaya right away. Khadijah is really concerned about that."

"Done, what have you found out?"

"I'm working on this around the clock, nothing yet."

I wasn't trying to hear that shit; the rat couldn't be that hard to find. I need to get to Samaya and get ready to get the kids and Nita out of here. After that, I'll be able to set the streets on fire and know that they won't be at risk of being caught up in our shit. Preston attempted to assure me that he is on his job, but until Khadijah walk out that bitch or he give me some information so that I can assist, he ain't doing it good enough for me.

"I'll be in touch, I have to take this call," I said before switching over to Mayhem.

"I need you to get up to the hospital, don't tell Nita. I got fucking shot."

"I'm on my way," I said as I snatched up my coat and keys and damn near ran out the house.

As if we don't have enough shit going on; I'm surprised the muthafucka didn't think I was involved. Who the fuck could coming at him unless he back on some bullshit. I'm trying to give him the benefit of the doubt because I know that he should understand the severity of what the fuck is going on around us right now. My brother can't get right, and right now I don't have time for no unnecessary bullshit.

As I made my way to the hospital my phone started ringing it was Alicia. I saw her at Killa's funeral and we've been talking and texting when I have time. Honestly, I'm surprised that she's even willing to talk to me. I was wrong for the way that I did her, and the way shit turned out with Evelynn and I was the karma that I wasn't expecting or prepared for. Alicia has been the only peace that I have had in the past few weeks besides my kids. I'm keeping her at a distance because trusting a woman isn't something that I don't think right now I can do.

I let Alicia go to voicemail and made my way into the hospital. I zipped up my coat while checking my gun. I don't put shit past anybody, and today isn't going to be my day to go without a mutha-fucking fight. The woman at the front desk pointed me in the direction of Mayhem's room and I noticed Trina's delusional ass sitting in the waiting room. I never met somebody that only shows up when a nigga is on his deathbed. I haven't seen this bitch in years, but she shows up, every time this nigga gets shot. Trina and her sister neither one of them ain't shit and even though they have different mothers I have to believe that that shit is somewhere deep in their blood.

"The only person that knew where I was at was Steel," Mayhem said as soon as the door shut behind me.

"Well, that's our fucking brother he wouldn't have shot you or had nobody shot you. That's some shit that you would do," I said.

"I know, but I'm just trying to figure out who the fuck else would have tried this shit. We have to hit the block tonight! Once they come back in here nigga we got to get out here! Waiting another minute is going to have us dead or gone forever, nigga!"

"You ready?" I asked.

"Nigga, I stay ready," Mayhem said cocking his gun back.

I know that I didn't shoot at Mayhem, but the look he is giving me has me wondering if he knows that. I really don't have time to go to war and shit without Killa I really don't know who the fuck I can trust. I sent a text to Lynn, telling her I had a job for her tonight. Before Mayhem and I hit the streets, I need to handle some shit in one of the neighborhoods that we control. Ivy came into the hospital room and Mayhem and I agreed to get with each other after midnight to handle what needed to be handled together. I left out so that I could go and meet Lynn.

~

As Lynn and I approached the block on Harley Davidson; for it to be fall it's hot as hell and it's a lot of witnesses, but that exactly why I wanted Lynn on the back of my bike. They can't see my face because of my helmet but they can see Lynn's white face and blonde hair and that's exactly how the news will describe it in the morning. Clearly, the nigga that I got running this block have forgotten their fucking job; as soon as time permits they will be getting replaced. Right now, I don't have time for that, but these off brand niggas that have just set up shop they got to go this shit mine. I'll be damn if anybody gone work on this muthafucka that I didn't authorize. As Soon as we turned the corner Lynn started to shoot, hitting them niggas one by one.

I came to a stop, so I could hit the last nigga that I had given instructions to Lynn to leave for me to get. I was told by Bizzie that he was supposed to be the leader that had already been warned once to get the fuck off the block.

"Listen Bro, I'll leave. I'll give you everything I got—"

It was too late for that shit, that little money he was getting was the least of my concerns. I didn't want that or that cheap ass jewelry he was offering. I let off a few rounds into his body and cut his throat so deep that his head was damn near detached from his body. I needed to send a message I needed niggas to know that I'm not playing and at this point nobody is safe. Lynn and I made our way to one of our spots. I changed my clothes and gave Lynn the rest of her payment and made sure she knew to be on standby in case I needed her for anything else.

I don't know what the fuck Rossi, could be calling me for he promised me that had Evelynn under control and he would make her suffer for everything that she has done for the rest of life. He not calling to give me free bricks so, what the fuck could we need to discuss. I just let the phone ring until it went to voicemail. Somebody was knocking at the door I know its Mayhem. High off pain pills and liquor, I know he out his mind, but tonight that will come in handy because I been out of mine for a while.

"Nigga you ready," Mayhem said with his arm in a fucking sling and a blunt hanging out of his mouth."

I cocked my berretta and we made our way to his car. The look that's in his eyes I haven't seen since September 9th. I'm not sure if that hate that I feel coming from him is for me or our enemies. Shit. It's probably a combination. Right now, my brother is all that I have, and I know that I am all that he has.

Mayhem's phone started ringing and mine started bussing at the same damn time. He turned down Bossie that was banging through his Monte Carlo speakers. It was Nita calling me, she been nervous and worrying about everything that's going on, so I'm not surprised that she's calling.

"Messiah! They just picked up Ivy!" Nita screamed on the phone as soon as the call connected.

"Calm down, Nita I'll handle it. I'm going to make sure that he gets out."

How the hell would she know that he was locked up? She hates that nigga just as much as I hate Evelynn. Nita is still crying and screaming in my ear. Mayhem is on the phone talking calm to whoever he is on the phone with but the way this nigga is driving he is just as fucked up as Nita is. I ensured my momma for the hundredth time I was on it and got her off the phone.

"Nigga you alright? Don't kill me. We supposed to be handling these niggas tonight," I said.

"Nigga, I'm not but they got Ivy as I see Nita just told you. Somebody on the inside is telling. Not only do we got to take care of all these muthafuckas that you thought it was a good idea to let live but somebody in the family got to go to!"

Ivy hasn't done shit in years but help us, but the only people that know that is us. This shit with Mayhem and I got him looking at me crazy. I know why, but when Ivy reminded us of why we needed each I thought that we were both on the same page, but I got to watch my back with this nigga too. Even though I didn't let Mayhem know that I was watching these niggas, but I have been. I knew in the back of mind one day they might be a problem, but Ivy always told me there was no reason to catch bodies until they started to talk and clearly if this nigga ain't talking then he can lead me to the bitch that is. Fucking with Lay was one of the biggest mistakes that I ever made but shit I got to deal with that shit now and that bitch will be handled alone.

Mayhem kicked in the door on the first try and the door smacked the floor. If anybody is sleep in this muthafucka they woke now. This nigga Ray was sitting on the couch with a bitch on top of him. The bitch jumped off begging for her life and I put a bullet in her head silencing her before she could finish her sentence. Mayhem made his way through the house.

"So, you caught a case and you telling now?" I asked.

"Naw man, I told yo brother I would never tell—" Ray said as I shot him in his arm.

This nigga was going to feel every bit of me tonight, so this was going to be nice and slow. I looked back and looked at Mayhem, he nodded his head so nobody else was in the house. This nigga is going to give up everything before he goes because the other nigga that robbed me and they whole muthafucking families are gone tonight. If they not gone tonight I will not sleep until all of them are gone. Mayhem lit another blunt and was leaning against the wall. I know a lot, but I need this nigga to tell everything I may not have noticed because that will be the only thing to keep us free. I keep thinking about my Harmony and Messiah Jr and for them, I will do whatever it takes to make sure that we are good forever and after this, I'm out the game for good!

We were taught that this life was okay, but the weight that I hold on my shoulders and looking at my son I know that I have to make a change to make sure that my kids never know anything about this lifestyle. I was taught this shit was acceptable. I remember having an extra laundry room with guns and bricks in the washer; that I was told never to go into, that why my kids will never know that life.

"So, who the fuck is talking!" I demanded answers because this nigga know.

"It's Lay nigga just let me go, she got yo sonnnn.. fuck! Get that bitch. I wooould never tell on you. I got a family, I knowww who y'all is and I would never risk their life over—" Ray, attempted to say before that burning hit his bitch ass.

I can't believe this shit and the way Mayhem was chocking he was surprised too. Damn so. This bitch thought it was okay to just hide my baby. The pain that I'm feeling with Evelynn, is damn near tripled with another baby that I feel like I abandoned. I missed the moments that I got with Harmony. I feel like a real bitch ass nigga; even though my dad wasn't able to be there due to him being killed Ivy was there every step of the way. I promised myself I was going to play the game the right way, the way that Ivy and my momma taught me, so my seeds would never see that life.

I had to push my feelings to the side and let another shot off in Ray, so he would tell everything I needed to know. Just like I knew, he ran down everything. The most important thing was where did Lay lay her head, so I could get my fucking son. As he began to beg for his life I let off more shots than they did when they hit Bonnie and Clyde. This nigga had to go, just like Ivy taught me. You only kill when necessary and when dealing with Arapahoe county this nigga had to go even if he ain't talking now when looking at a judge and facing hundreds of years who knows what the fuck he might have told.

As we made our way out the house Mayhem damn near fell off the porch tripping over a rock that was there as decoration, but I noticed something is taped to it. It was a small envelope with keys in it. I took it just in case grabbed my burner to call Chaos to get this cleaned up because it's going to be a long night.

"Nigga bring yo ass on I don't have all night," I said.

This nigga on the phone arguing with a bitch. I don't have time for this shit tonight. Those days when we were up for two to three days at a time are back. Christmas is in less than a month and I'll be damned if I'm not with my kids on Christmas morning. Mayhem cripple ass insisted on driving.

"I got to get rid of Trina," Mayhem said as got in the car.

FIVE

# Messiah

---

$\mathcal{N}$ita had been in charge of the majority of my legal businesses from the beginning. Evelynn didn't want to, and I had to have somebody that I trust watching everything. Now with everything that has gone down, it was good that Nita was in charge. Nita and I were meeting with Preston and aunt Tina is watching the kids.

"So, what is going on with Ivy? When are, you getting him out?" Nita asked.

"Nita, I don't think that Ivy is going to be getting out. He asked for me to give you this," Preston said while pushing a manila envelope across the table.

Nita jumped up from her chair and started beating on the table. Her face had turned red and even had tears falling from her face. Preston was scared as fuck, but I know my momma ain't going to do nothing to him.

"Why M? Why? You got to do something! You got to make this right! After all, Ivy has done for you and this family" Nita screamed, as her tears just continued to fall.

I feel bad enough and all the shit that is going on is already on my fucking back, and nothing has changed I have to be the one to make everything right. Nita snatched the envelope off the table and pushed it into her purse and walked out of Preston's office. Not before knocking everything on her way to the floor and slamming the door so hard that the windows shook. Nita isn't the type of mom that wants you to console her when shit like this is going down. I have to be the man that she raised me to be and make shit right. She's going to talk shit and cause hell until everything is the way that she wants it to be.

"I know that you all are going through some horrible times right now and I don't know how to tell you this, but your brother Steel is the one that the feds have. He started off telling on his wife and now Ivy. He could be coming for the rest of you any day now."

"Let Ivy and Khadijah know that whatever they need it's done," I said as I got up to leave while handing Preston an envelope.

Every other client was going to have to be placed on the back-burner. Right now, his job is to eat, shit, and sleep working on this shit. If anything is happening, he needs to know before it happens. I'm not going to jail, I don't have time for that. The money that he doesn't have to report to the IRS will be all the motivation he needs to keep the rest of us fucking free. When I tell Nita and Mayhem that Steel is telling, I don't know how the fuck they're going to take it but shit this is what it is!

Once I made it to the car Nita was leaning against it on the phone and she rushed whoever she was talking to off the phone. The pain and hurt in Nita's eyes, I couldn't take looking at her right now, so I just kept my eyes on the road.

"I just talked to Ivy, we need to kill Steel," Nita said, turning towards me.

"We not doing anything, I got it."

As we pulled up to the house Mayhem was getting out of his car. Nita jumped out slamming my door shattering my window like I told on Ivy. I made a call to get my window fixed Mayhem and I needed to talk right now. I went in to check on Lil'M, he is gaining weight more quickly then they figured he would and his breathing has improved a lot as well. Aunt Tina and Harmony were sitting in the room with him.

"Dad! Can we go home now? Is mommy back yet?" Harmony screamed as I walked in the room.

My momma decided to tell her that she was on a trip and ever since she keeps asking when she is coming back. I wish that we could just go home, and shit was less hectic, but I faced the fact that we can't go home and never will be able to. I just had to have a talk with Nita because they have to get the fuck out of here. The longer we wait the more shit that can happen.

"Nita, we need to talk," I said as I walked into the living room.

"What's wrong now? What the fuck else can possibly go wrong?" Nita said, then downed a shot.

"I need you to take the kids and leave right after Christmas. I'll be coming shortly after, but we can't stay here. None of us know what the fuck is about to happen, and Steel knows everyt—"

"What the fuck did you just say?" Mayhem screamed.

"Steel is the one that is working with the people," I said turning to face Mayhem.

This is something that could easily tear us apart, but I've had a getaway plan for years. I always knew this wasn't going to last forever. I just never knew that my brother would be what attempted to tear us apart.

# Mayhem

I heard M and I knew that he wasn't the one talking. I may not fuck with him like that, but we share the same blood. We might go to war with each other but working with the feds is something that we would never do. I can't believe Steel though, a muthafucka that will tell on his own dad ain't shit and ain't no way around it. If he will tell on his wife and dad shit, he doesn't give a fuck about anything.

"What about B and Miracle?" Nita asked.

Miracle is for sure going, but B I might have to fuck around and kill Arie about that. I have to go and meet her. She wants to talk all of a sudden. They dropped the case for burning down my house, why I don't know, so unless it has something to do with B we don't have anything to talk about.

"We need to go around to the hiding spots and clean them all out too," I said.

I have been watching this nigga M like a hawk and I know that we have to work together to be able to come from under all this, but something is telling me that I can't trust him. At the end of the day, muthafuckas are going to look out for themselves first and that's with anybody.

"Nita, text Trina a picture of Miracle because that's the closest she going to get to her," I said.

"B and Arie need to just come with me Mayhem."

I heard Nita but I'm not trying to hear that shit, fuck Arie. She crossed the line; she did some shit that I would have killed the next bitch about. If I said I didn't want to still kill the bitch I would be lying it's just some people that need to die before her. Messiah phone started ringing and he got up to leave the room.

"Who is that? This is important, we need to talk," Nita said.

"It's Alicia, momma damn give me a second.

Now is not the time for this nigga to be falling in love with another bitch. Nita was talking to me, but I 'm not trying to hear anything she has to say about Arie and that bitch ain't coming. I just know that she not about to let me just take B and I wouldn't want him to just never be able to see his mom again. Our problems with each other don't have anything to do with him.

"Did you tell M, that you were back fucking with Ivy?"

"It ain't none of y'all business what the fuck I do. I'm y'all momma!"

"I'll be back since you got time to break for love! I screamed down the hall where M was at.

"Will you think about talking to Arie, for me Maurice. If we can never come back here. We all need to be together,"

I made my way out the house I need to talk to Arie whether I want to or not. Arie never did any dirt with me, but she used the money that I made from the streets, so she needs to know that they could be coming for her too. I don't wish being locked up on anybody, but if she doesn't say the right thing she will get sent to her maker without a problem.

Arie did all that moving shit for nothing. Bitch you ain't in the witness protection program what the fuck makes you think I'm not going to find out where you live. As I pulled up to Arie's and got out of the car. When I put my key in the door to unlock it I felt somebody pulling the door open.

"How the fuck—" Arie screamed.

"Girl shut the fuck up, we need to talk."

I walked around Arie and made my way through the house. I'm going to try to talk to her and not cuss her ass out but who knows how the fuck this is going to go. I took a deep breath and turned to face her, and she is crying sitting on the couch.

"What's wrong A?"

"It doesn't fucking matter, what the fuck do you want?"

"I'm going to try not to cuss you the fuck out cuz if I didn't care I wouldn't have fucking asked, and you know that."

I made my way out of the room to go and see B, so she could get herself together. Since she doesn't want to talk to me about her problems. She can go and sit and talk to that nigga Killa at his grave if she would like too. I got too much other shit going on to be arguing with Arie about some shit that doesn't even matter anymore.

B is sleep, so I just left him alone and turned off his tv, when I turned around Arie was standing in the doorway. I took her through a lot of shit and for that I was wrong, but I can't take any of that shit back. I accepted the fact that I pushed her too far and that's why she's done with me. I just can't accept the fact that she fucked Killa. It could have been anybody else in the world, but damn Killa. We had some good times and shit wasn't always bad, she stayed down on days when the next bitch would have left my ass. I closed B's door behind me.

"Mayhem will you stay here tonight."

"Why you don't want to mourn yo man Killa?"

Arie rolled her eyes and walked away.

# Arie

I don't know why I even asked Mayhem to stay here and thought that he would drop everything and be here for me. I thought that things might have changed with Steel and my situation. He is saying everything that I really wish that Mayhem would say to me. Windows keep getting busted out. Bitches have been calling playing on my phone; showing up to my shop and shit; as if I don't have enough going on there. The contractors go from going to be done by the end of the week to they need more money and more time.

When it came to certain shit I was always able to depend on Mayhem to get shit done. I need that rock now more than ever. All of a sudden whenever Steel is around he wants to discuss Mayhem. One thing that will turn me off quick from any man, is being concerned about the next man. I never had that problem with Steel before he didn't give a fuck about Lunatic or any other nigga. Now all of a sudden, he just wants to sit for hours and talk about Mayhem and Messiah. Just when I thought that for once things might be different it's some bullshit. My phone started ringing it was Steel, I walked out of the living room where Mayhem was sitting down flipping through channels.

"I'm not going to be able to come something came up?" Steel said, as soon as the phone connected.

"I'll be over first thing in the morning. You know the situation with Khadijah. My daughter is sick, and I promise, I'll be over there first thing in the morning,"

"Okay cool. I ain't tripping. I understand."

Forever I wanted Steel all to myself, but I just played my role and kept things how they were because it was either that or nothing at all. Now that we are supposed to be together and he talks about all these plans of us getting married and having a family, but I don't think I want it anymore with him. I want Mayhem, and nobody will be ever to ever take his place. I can't stand Mayhem and I know he feels the same about me, but I know Mayhem. I thought I knew Steel, but his bitch tendencies aren't something that I'm willing to deal with.

"Look Arie, the feds are coming down on us and I need to get B out of here so none of this shit will affect him," Mayhem blurted out as I walked back into the room.

"What's going on?"

I know the lifestyle that we lived and I'm not saying that it's okay and that there is no better way to make it out the hood, but it's what worked to get us out. I know that Mayhem has done a lot of wrongs and for years I was down with whatever he said or wanted because I knew that when he made moves in the streets that he would always make sure that B and I were going to be okay. The fact that it has just turned into B kind of hurts. What the fuck about me? If the feds are coming to town they could be coming for me too.

"What the fuck about me?"

"Look Arie, I'm not begging or kissing yo ass to come. The day after Christmas Nita is leaving with the kids. Have B ready and if yo ass wants to stay here then fuck it," Mayhem said and got up to leave.

I got up and followed in behind Mayhem, I didn't want him to go but I'll be damned if I beg him to stay. I have been trying to convince myself that I need to be done with Mayhem and attempting to use other people as a replacement, but with his crazy no good ass I want him here now more than ever.

"I'll be muthafucking back in a few hours," Mayhem said before the door shut in my face.

I grabbed my kindle and laid on the couch. I haven't read in forever and I need to catch up on my reading and relax. My phone started ringing and I looked at it, it was an unknown number again. I had been ignoring these calls because when they call they don't say shit but breathe. I decided to answer and see if they had something to say tonight.

"So, I see you made up with your man if you could have played yo fucking position a long time ago this could have been a lot smoother," the unknown bitch said.

"Who the fuck is this?"

"Bitch it doesn't matter it will be in your best interest to stay with Mayhem or I'll kill you and ya son bitch!"

Click.

I got up, to go look outside and see if I saw any cars that I didn't recognize but I didn't. I went upstairs to my closet to get a gun. It's going to be a long night, but maybe Mayhem is right B and I do need to leave with Nita. Using the money made me just as guilty, and I'm not going to jail for anybody. Then I have to think about Steel, am I willing to walk away when he is standing in front of me offering all of him.

∽

"Why the fuck are you down here? Why the fuck are you sleeping with a gun?" Mayhem asked while laying a cover over me.

I didn't answer him fast enough because he just started going the fuck off. With me not talking to him unless I absolutely have to, I have no idea what's really going on. I still don't even know what the fuck happened to Killa. I can't ask Mayhem that though, he still in his feelings about me fucking with him. A nigga can fuck up too many times to count but a woman is supposed to stay down forever and if she doesn't she ain't shit. I fuck one nigga and I'm the worst bitch he ever met in all his life.

"Mayhem, will you just be real with me and tell me what's going on?" I said as I sat up on the couch.

"Look Steel, is working with the feds we don't know what else he's going to tell."

Mayhem was still telling me everything but after he said that Steel was working with the feds nothing else mattered. I can't tell Mayhem the truth about Steel and me. I never told anybody the truth about us. The fact that I got with Mayhem knowing that I had fucked with Steel before him he'll never forgive me. While Mayhem is talking to me I'm just trying to remember anything that I might have said to Steel that could be used against us all.

"Did Steel tell on Khadijah?"

"Yea, so if he told her then we all can go," Mayhem said, shrugging his shoulders.

I sent Steel a text telling him I had a family emergency and needed to leave town for a few days and I would call him when I got to Arizona. The look Mayhem has in his eyes I have seen many times before. One thing I know for sure is that it's going to be a lot of bodies dropping and I just pray that for the sake of B, that I'm not one of them.

# Trina

I looked across the street at Arie's house and saw Mayhem's car parked in the driveway. I'm waiting for Steel to pull up so that we can talk about how the fuck he didn't kill Mayhem. Just so happened one of my aunts live across the street from where Arie moved, so I was able to know when Arie came and went. Mayhem has Miracle and is still mad at me. This is nothing new if you don't do what Mayhem says or say something that Mayhem does not like then he will make sure that you see how he got the name Mayhem.My dad is calling, now is really not a good time, but I answered anyway.

"Trina, get here right now." My father said, calmly but I know him well enough to know that there is a problem and he hung up before I could even respond.

I made my way out to my car, so I could hurry up and get back to meet Steel. Maybe there are some issues with my cousin Candy and he needs to me step up now. I just hope that it is something that can be handled quick and fast because I have enough shit to worry about besides family issues.

I jumped out of my car and my father met me at the door. The look in his eyes I have never seen before, and I could feel the rage oozing from him. His skin is red as if he was sunburned, but there is no way that is the reason why he is so red.

"Dad, what's wrong?"

"Trina, go into the house."

When I walked into the house my brother Rossi Jr started smiling but it wasn't the type of warm smile that you would give someone when you are happy to see someone it was the type of smile that the devils give you when you first get to hell. He has always hated me, so this is nothing new. He feels entitled to be the one to take over the family business, but even if I never get it; dad will give it to a stranger before he gives it to him.

"Dad, what is —" I attempted to say before, I was smacked to the ground from the back and smacked the marble floors.

"What the fuck have you told Sharief?" Rossi asked still in a calm tone.

Rossi is the type of man he doesn't have to yell. The fear that he puts in people is enough. He has plenty of people that will reach out and touch you if they think that you have done him wrong. I can remember one time in my life when he disciplined me. Why would he care what I discussed with Sharief? I have to be careful what I tell him because if I tell him the wrong thing I'll feel his wrath even more. I was trying

"Speak, Trina," Rossi said losing his patience.

"I just was asking him he could talk to Mayhem for me, we haven't been getting along lately."

"You have one more chance to tell me the truth," my father said pulling out a gun and placing it in the middle of my forehead.

"Wait, wait, wait," I pleaded.

"You have decided to bring in a federal informant into my business," Rossi said.

I don't know what to say. There is no way that Steel could be snitching and if he is then that means that he could be cooperating against Mayhem and Messiah as well. He must have been trying to set me up from the beginning.

"Tell me everything and don't leave anything out," Rossi said with the gun still to my head.

# Evelynn

As a kid, I always wondered what my mom would be like. How did she wear her hair? What was her favorite color? Did she look like me? Is she allergic to the same things I am? Now as I look at Saadiya, I'm happy that she decided to leave me at the fucking fire station. Rossi has me in this house with her. She's been in this house for years and I haven't even wasted my time trying to get her to run with me. She is terrified of Rossi and his henchmen who are never too far away.

Rossi comes here every so often. He has ordered his men to beat both of us at least once a day. We can't leave the house and they allow us to eat once a day. I never appreciated Messiah as much as I do right now. I keep trying to think of a way that I can get out of here. Big Moe is here in the morning and then there is Syke that comes in the afternoon. Syke doesn't watch us as carefully as Moe does. So, if I'm going to take a run for it, it will have to be when Syke is here.

Saadiya is cold she does not have the warmth and loving aroma that I received from momma Janice. Every once in a while, I catch her just staring at me, but she hardly says more than few words to me.

"I did everything I could to make sure that Rossi never found you. So, you wouldn't have to pay for what I did," Saadiya blurted out.

I didn't know what to say. I just had to go after the dope boy and he just so happened to be doing business with the father I never knew. I rubbed my fingertips across the scars that are now covering my body and started to think about Harmony and my baby boy that will never know who I am. I never wanted my kids to go through anything that I did and to always know that no matter what I loved them, and I would be there. If I ever get out of here Messiah isn't going to let me see the kids, and if I even try to get close to them he'll kill me.

"You have another roommate," Rossi said as Rossi Jr flung Trina into the wall of the living room. We weren't living in a bad neighborhood or the worst house ever. It actually reminded me a lot of the home that I shared with Messiah. The neighbors would never know what is going on inside this house.

Rossi and Rossi jr left out just as fast as they came in. Saadiya grabbed me by arm snatching me off the couch and ushering me out the living room. As soon as we were far enough away that Trina couldn't hear us Saadiya started whispering "You don't have to believe anything that I say, but yo ass better listen when I say do not trust that bitch. She'll do anything to get over on anybody and that ain't yo fucking sister because Rossi isn't yo fucking dad; Moretti is." Saadiya just walked away and left me standing there. Whoever the fuck my dad is really doesn't make any difference now, they missed everything. I can't get back the time that whoever my father is missed.

I have to get the fuck out of here. When I leave here, I won't have anything I'll be starting all over from the bottom. I have to be able to get out of here to get to Messiah's money and I'll just fucking leave town. I have no family that I can go to or nobody that would even think about helping me. Right now, I'm all I have and even though I don't really know Saadiya I know that Trina working with me to get out of here isn't going to work either. Messiah and Mayhem hate her just as much as me.

# SIX

# Messiah

"*M*, are you done yet?" Nita screamed from down the hall.

I love my momma, but she damn loud and she can't just talk regular, she got to scream. The little bit of sleep I finally got, it still didn't make a difference. If I got to stay up for days to make sure that their good, then that's what I'll have to do. I know that Nita trying to wake up the kids, so they can open their gifts instead of letting them sleep like I said to.

Arie came walking out of the room she's been staying in. I still can't believe that Mayhem brought her here. I know that he wants B to go with Nita, but I don't know how the fuck that's going to work.

"Messiah! Arie! Come here right now!" Nita yelled.

"Yes, Nita the kids can come down," I yelled up the stairs.

Arie and I were both standing at the bottom of the stairs. B and Harmony both made their way downstairs. Nita came down right after them. The look on her face I could tell that her holiday cheer had gone out the window, and its some more bullshit. I thought just one day that I could relax and not have to worry about no bullshit but that is just asking for too much, I guess.

"They are at Mayhem's condo downtown to arrest him, I'm going down there now," Nita said while putting on her coat.

"Hold on, wait I'm coming with you," Arie said.

I made my way onto the living room, so I could see the look on the kid's face as they open all their gifts. Messiah Jr just barely went back to sleep, he isn't old enough to even know or understand what's going on. Thankfully he's progressing well enough so that Nita can take him, so I know that they will be safe, and the feds won't be able to get close to Nita. Alicia is on her way over here. I was hesitant to get close to anybody after all the bullshit that I went through with E, but with Alicia, I can tell that she is not on no bullshit.

It's crazy how after so long and with all the things that have changed it's like we never missed a beat. I didn't think that Alicia would forgive me for what I did to her, but she isn't bitter. My burner rang, and I answered without checking to see who it is.

"Yea," I said.

"Merry Christmas, the kids up yet?" Ivy said.

"Merry Christmas; yea their opening their gifts."

This was the first Christmas I've ever had without my whole family around me. If there was anything that could be done so that Ivy could be released, then it would have been done. Ivy keeps talking that shit about not worrying about him and do what I must do for the kids and Nita. Ivy gave me the address where Steel may be at. We've been looking high and low for him. I got some niggas sitting outside of Dijah's sister's house if he was to go by and get the kids, but he hasn't been there either. If this nigga goes, so does this case that is coming for all of us.

"Has Nita opened that envelope?" Ivy asked.

"I don't know."

"Y'all, need to open it together."

"Let me talk to Harmony and B."

I gave B the phone and went to answer the door it must be Alicia. Alicia has been my peace since she been back around. I just don't want to bring her into my bullshit. She keeps saying that she doesn't care and she's down to ride with me regardless of what's going on and what might come. I took the bags filled with gifts out

Alicia's hands and she wrapped her arms around my neck and kissed me.

Alicia is beautiful, caramel complexion, shoulder-length hair. She has brown eyes and she's thick as fuck. Outside of how bad she is on the outside; inside she's loyal, understanding and she is the girl that I let get away. That is now a full-grown woman and I'll never let her get away again.

"Dad!" Harmony screamed as she came running up to us.

I turned around towards Harmony and tears filled my baby's eyes and she took off running away from us. My baby knows that Alicia isn't her mom and even with her being so young she knows that something is going on with her mom and me because of how long it has been since she saw her. Alicia followed me into the living room where B was at still opening gifts. I made my way to check on my baby.

"Harmony."

I walked into her room and she was sitting on her bed, holding one of her teddy bears. I know that one day I'll have to explain to Harmony about what happened with E and me. I have never wanted anything I do to affect Harmony. I make moves always thinking of her first.

"Dad, is mommy coming back?"

"No, but she loves you and your baby brother. Ya mom made some bad choices—"

Harmony just started to cry harder while squeezing me as tight as she could.

# Arie

---

"Mam, I'm not going to ask you again to step back," an officer said to Nita.

I was looking around the apartment for the book that Mayhem told me to get before he was taken away in the squad car. These dumb muthafuckas wouldn't have opened it. I found it and put it into my bag and pulled Nita's crazy ass out of here before she went to jail on Christmas day too.

"Fuck you bitches, my coat costs more than y'all fucking salary!" Nita screamed.

She just had to say something else. I have been through this before with Mayhem and some way somehow, he always comes home. I can feel in my heart that this time is different and the fact that there is nothing that I can do that will make things any different. Since Mayhem showed up at my house, the next day B and I moved in with Nita and the kids. I had to pick a side and stay there. I know one thing for sure whether Mayhem is locked up or not I'll always be good if I am on his side.

I couldn't tell Mayhem about Steel and me. It's killing me being around Nita and the rest of the family. If I tell them it's a chance that I'll be dead before I tell them everything, but not telling them is killing me more and more every day. The only two people who know where I am at is Tiara and my momma. B didn't care where we lived if Mayhem was there. Mayhem being away again isn't going to be easy for him.

Nita slammed the car into park and I looked up, but we weren't at the hideout. We are at her mom's house that I didn't think anybody lived in anymore.

"Bitch, get yo ass out this car and come on!" Nita screamed while getting out the car.

I got out the car and made my way into the house. Nita was looking for something, I could hear her, and shit being thrown around. Nita came back into the room with two hammers.

"Here girl, what the fuck are you waiting for?" Nita said, handing me a hammer.

"What am I supposed to do with this?"

"Its money in every room of this house and Mayhem didn't make it over her to get it. The big money is in the walls; every wall with a picture of Messiah or Mayhem hanging on it. Hurry up girl I don't have all fucking day."

Nita threw a roll of garbage bags at me. I made my way through the house and got the money. Nita and I met back up downstairs and made our way out. We rode in silence back to the house. I wanted to tell Nita about Steel and me, but I just couldn't do it.

"Arie are you coming with us?" Nita asked, breaking the silence.

"Yea."

I don't know if I'm going or not. I don't know if I can look all of them in the face knowing what role that I could have played in all that is happening to them right now. My phone started ringing its Steel. I haven't talked to him since Mayhem told me about the real him. I don't know what to say to him.

The game that we played years ago was safe for me it worked. Even though it was wrong on both of our parts neither one of us cared and the only thing that stopped us was the judge that sent Steel away. With all that was going on in my life when I saw Steel at the hospital, I just ran towards what I knew too well. I fucked up and got to take that shit. I can't blame Mayhem or nobody else for this. Steel was an addiction that I was forced to break, but as soon as he was back in the picture I had to have him, and it didn't matter the consequences.

I feel so uncomfortable being around the family. This has been my family forever and I feel like somebody knows my secret that I have been able to hide forever. Walking into the house and seeing Alicia calmed my nerves a little. Mayhem told me that Alicia was back in the picture. After all the shit that Evelynn did to him, I'm surprised that he can trust any female again.

"Wassup Arie?" Alicia said.

"Hey, girl."

Alicia loved Messiah more than life itself. So, when he decided that after taking her through hell and back when we were teenagers and leaving her that shit broke her down bad. Alicia and I knew each other but we were never that close, but everybody could see the drastic change in her while she was dealing with her heartbreak. Shit, it looks like that heart is mended and she right back in love like she never left.

"Arie, can I talk to you for a second," Alicia said as she walked towards me.

"Yea, what's up?"

As we made our way out the room I started to think about what the fuck she could want to talk to me about. I can't give anybody any love advice. Shit, the only reason why I'm here is that I felt safe being around Mayhem. Now Mayhem isn't here I feel like a fucking stranger.

"I know we never really been real close, but I just have to ask somebody and you all I got in this house that will possibly not lie to me but is —"

"Messiah is no longer with E. She's gone and isn't coming back."

I could see that she calmed down after I said that, meanwhile I don't know what the fuck I should do. I need to get the fuck out here and go see T. It's going to kill me to tell her, but I know that no matter what she won't turn her back on me and will still be here whenever I need her.

"Nita, I have to go check on my mom and I'll be right back."

"B can stay. Tell yo momma I said hi."

I got my ass in the car and made my way to T's. I know she is at home because it's her off day. My mom is down south with her sister for Christmas, so I can't go over there. I can already hear what she would have to say if I told her about Steel. My mom likes Mayhem because he was able to provide and wasn't beating my ass like Loon. Mayhem has a good heart to those that he loves and fucks with but for the others, he will set it the fuck off at your momma's funeral.

I ran into Tiara's and let myself in using my key. Just like I figured she was sitting in the living room watching Real House Wives of Atlanta and smoking a blunt. I made myself at home and went to look for a drink. She had a bottle of Remy and Red Bull, I'm going to need this whole bottle to make it through this Christmas.

"Bitch, what the fuck is wrong with you?"

"T, look it's a lot of shit that I haven't told you, but I have to tell somebody."

I took the fifth to the head and then ran down everything that has been killing me. T was so damn shocked she was letting the blunt just burn and that is something her ass will never do. I took the blunt from her and hit it a few times and just started to pour out my heart and soul to the only person that I can.

"Bitch, how the fuck you didn't tell me this shit. Hoe I tell yo ass everything!" T screamed in between taking the bottle to the head.

Tiara is right we have told each other everything since the seventh grade. I didn't want anybody to know what I was doing. Even though T knew everything that I was going through with Loon; I was still fucking with somebody's husband. I couldn't tell anybody until now and that is only because I must accept the fact that I was wrong and shit even though at the time it felt so right, just to get away from what I was dealing with at home. Khadijah was probably at home waiting for Steel to come home while my legs were to the headboard at the Hilton.

"That nigga Steel is crazy girl and you already knew that. I don't give a fuck if he is telling or not. He not just going to walk away quietly, and you know that. Who the fuck is this at my door it better not be fucking Dirt! I'm done with his black ass!"

She is always done with Dirt. After all these years they still find their way back to each other. When I was crying and whining over Mayhem she was doing the same for Dirt. I better get ready to take my ass back to my hideout because if that's Dirt I'm getting kicked out.

"Girl, move the fuck out of my way! I know she's in here," Steel yelled; damn near knocking T over.

"Muthafucka, this is my house and what you won't be doing is bringing yo ass in here trying to run shit!" Tiara screamed, coming right behind Steel.

"Arie, we need to talk," Steel spat.

I just kept sitting on the couch drinking. Shit, I already got in bed with a rat and we couldn't have shit to talk about. I'm sure the feds already heard everything I said and they just waiting to come looking for me. At least I'll be able to write Mayhem while I do my time. This nigga never loved me and the way he's looking at me I should have known it from the beginning I wasn't anything but a nut.

"Girl, if you don't get yo ass; off that muthafucking couch and come outside."

T was cussing Steel out but this muthafucka didn't care. He made his way out the house and I got my ass off the couch with the Remy and made my way out too.

"I'm going to get my gun!" T screamed before the door closed behind me.

It's nothing that Steel can say to make shit right. He always knew what to say to make something that was wrong feel so right. He fucked and sucked every worry and pain that was in me out of me for so long. I choose the wrong niggas and it's nothing that I can do to change the shit now.

"Look, I know that you're mad, but you have to understand that I did everything that I did for us. So, we could finally be together and nothing or no one can stop it no."

I took the bottle to the head again. I heard everything that he was saying but none of that shit mattered anymore. How am I going to look B in the face and tell him that the only dad he has ever known is never coming back, and it's my fault too? I'm all cried out. I have been crying for days going into the bathroom sitting in the shower, so nobody would know.

"So, what we are supposed to just leave town and go live happily ever after?" I asked sarcastically.

"You have until Tomorrow morning at nine to meet me downtown at the Four Seasons, you can bring B, or you can leave him behind," Steel said pulling out his gun and laying it on his lap.

I took the bottle to head again and got out the car. So now I'm being forced into a relationship with a snitch. Every step that I took into the house I felt like it could easily be my last. I snatched the blunt out of Tiara's hand who is sitting on the porch with her gun on her lap. One thing is for sure I might have had to question a few bitches, but I will never have to question the love and loyalty that T and I have for each other. Bitches ain't shit they'll fuck yo nigga and come over and sit at yo table Sunday dinner, but with T, I never have to worry about no funny shit. I just hope that she'll understand why I can't do this shit anymore.

# Steel

"Where the fuck is my kids at?" I said while opening Samaya's mouth with my gun.

She has been spinning me about getting my kids since Khadija's trial is getting ready to start I have to go into protective custody around the clock after tonight. My kids are going with me and if Arie knows what's best she'll her ass to the room before the sun comes up in the morning. I've been through the house and my kids aren't here. This bitch has had them, and I know that she knows where the fuck they are at.

"I don't know where they are at somebody came in masked up and took them," Samaya managed to say.

I know Messiah and how he moves calculated with every step if I even try to get to my kids I'll be dead before I get close to them. I know that Messiah has his niggas ready to kill just because. I dropped Samaya on to the floor and she smacked the floor and could hear her neck break.

Messiah will tell my kids eventually that I'm a snitch and that's what they'll remember the most. He won't bother to tell them about the long nights on the block. The fact that I took the case when we all should have gone down. Fuck all of them none of them muthafuckas! None of them would have stood tall for me. Before I leave out I must make myself feel better and catch my last body because after tonight I'll be a citizen is some small city that I never heard of in Jackson Michigan. I put three bullets in Samaya's head and made my way outside.

"Get the fuck in the back of the car!" The guard that was supposed to be watching me said as he met me on the curb.

As I got into the back of the blacked-out town car; just like I figured Michelle was in the back seat. I'm sick of this bitch the only thing that she would be good for would be to fuck her in all three holes. This bitch just wants to bring Messiah down. Bitches get real bitter when you fuck them once and never call again.

"You have been meeting with the boss's daughter. When do you think that it would be a clever idea to have told me that? Especially considering the fact, that you have been picking and choosing when you want to wear yo wire."

I'm ready for this shit just to be over. I can't wait to just move on with my life; me and my bitch Arie. Once I got into the bed with this bitch it started off just wanting Messiah, but now clearly, she thinks that I'm fucking dumb. Cooperating against Rossi will have me and my momma dead. Even the witness protection won't be able to save me from them muthafuckas. Even though Trina's dumb ass told me a lot I'll never tell anybody damn sure not this bitch.

"I used to fuck the bitch; that's it and that's all. You think that muthafucka Rossi would let me get near him."

"I hope ya black ass is ready. If you fuck this up for me; I'll make sure that you get the death penalty."

"Bitch, I'm going to play my part," I said as I got out the car.

"One more thing, I'm picking up Nita next."

Nita was the mother to me that I never had. She made sure that I was good and never treated me any different than her sons. If one of us got something we all got it and if she beat one of our asses she beat all of them. I need to take my ass to sleep, what's done is done and soon I'll be off to my new life.

# Khadijah

"The kids are okay, Messiah has them," Preston whispered leaning over the table.

I could finally exhale. I know that M will make sure that my kids are okay and won't have to grow up being raised by the worst of the worst, a fucking federal informant. I know the time that I'm facing, and I'll take this shit. Hopefully one day I'm able to get out to be with my kids and if not, my kids will understand one day the thorough type of bitch that I am and no matter what. If you fuck up you got to deal with the consequences and no matter what, you never fold. The only regret that I have is not telling Messiah, but something in me was saying that Steel would take his time and not turn but shit that was clearly the dumb bitch that lives inside of all of us.

"Preston Look, I hear you but shit whatever is going to happen is going to happen. I just need you to get some money from M in here to me. I'll handle everything else just do what you can I guess."

I made my way to my phone to call my sister even though I paid that bitch for nothing; she's the only person right now that I can talk to. I tried to call Samaya and she didn't answer so I decided to call again.

"Hello," Some man said.

"Give Samaya the phone I don't have long."

"I'm sorry to tell you this mam, but Samaya is no longer with us. She was killed today. This is detective Rawls, are you some kin to Samaya?" Detective Rawls asked.

I know that bitch ass nigga Steel did this. The only thing we always had in common is the urge to kill and mine is killing me right now. I slammed the phone down and made my way back to my cell. I wanted to cry Samaya is all that I had besides my kids, and now she is gone. All because I wanted a man that could lead me and protect me, and, in the end, he just led me to this cell.

"Here Dijah, this is from Ivy," Mad Maxx the trustee said as she handed me a cellphone through the hole.

I went through the phone and it was a message from Ivy.

*I raised two real thorough men and they will be just fine in the free world, so I know that my grandkids will be just fine. So, keep yo fucking head up Dijah! Then I raised a selfish ass informant. I have to live with that I'll be good! I know that I taught him everything he needed to be able to make it even from behind the wall. He is weak and bitch like his momma and I always knew that shit. You didn't do anything wrong! Stand tall and that muthafucka will pay for what he has done!*

*IVY*

I could feel that shit in my soul and I could hear Ivy saying each word to me. I can finally talk to my kids. As the guard walked by me I could hear over the intercom, his ass being called to another unit, so I called Nita.

"Dijah were going to make it through this together," Nita said as soon as she answered.

"I know, Nita."

"Mom, Nana and Uncle Messiah explained everything to us; I understand," Sharieffa said.

I won't be able to see my baby off to prom. Go with her to colleges to decide which one that she wants to go to. That is something that will make my time even harder. As I explained the best way I could the reason for my decisions I started to think about my baby Lil' Sharief. I know that he'll be fine but not being able to be there with him to help him to become the solid man he needs to be is killing me on the inside. I laughed and smiled as I talked to my babies and made sure that they both know how much I love them. Even though Steel was away I didn't let that stop me from being the mother and wife that I always wished my own mother was.

Yea, I sold drugs and I was the best chef in the fucking west, but before anything else, I am a mother. I did what I did so that my kids could go down a different path. They won't have to move the way I did and live the life that I did. I know that the values and morals that I instilled in them will be used. That is the only thing that is keeping me alive and stopping me from balling up in a corner right now.

# Messiah

---

"I got to go handle something and I'll be back," I said as I put on my coat.

"Okay, I understand," Alicia said.

I kissed Alicia. The understanding and love of her is something that I haven't had since I left her. I've been dealing with a gimmie bitch for so long and I appreciate Alicia now more than I ever did. As soon as I finish up shit here I'm going to give her the happily ever after that I never gave her before. I need to go and get my son; I've been keeping a close eye on Lay. I know where she works and lives. I've also been keeping a close eye on my son. Through all the shit going on I managed to be able to make it to see him on a play date at Chucky Cheeses.

I've been switching out cars so much that I haven't even gotten the chance to figure out how a car works before I have to send it to be destroyed. I made my way to Lay's really quick. I have to get my son and make sure that he knows my side of the story.

I used my key and let myself into Lay's. She was sitting on the couch grading papers I assume since she's a middle school English teacher.

"O my god!" Lay screamed once she noticed me standing in the doorway.

I made my way across the room and sat down across from Lay on the love seat. I want to just kill this bitch. A little fun on the side just made me miss important times with my son. Looking at him, he looks just like me and there is no way that I could deny him even if I want to.

"Please, I promise that I won't tell just let me and my baby Amir go, please."

"Yo baby, hun? Yo mean my son that you have kept away from me and let him be around them broke ass, nothing ass niggas like Ray."

She doesn't know what to say and I can tell by the look in her eyes she never thought that I would show up on her doorstep. I have to live with myself for all the decisions that I have made. The good side of me wanted to just let her go and take my son. The gangsta in me knows that isn't possible. Ivy always told me to make sure that I finish my breakfast.

Lay closed her eyes still crying and began to pray, but it's too late and she should have thought about this. Mayhem wanted to kill her on September 9th, but I knew that she would never be threat. I know that even if I let her go she won't testify against us. She has to pay for the wrong that she has done. I put a bullet in her head and watched her neck snap back. I let a few more rounds off in her just to make sure the job is done.

I made my way through the house to get my son. He was still asleep, as I was snatching a few toys. I saw a picture of me and Lay in a frame; a picture that Lay and I took at the club. I don't even remember taking this picture with Lay. I snatcher the frame off the dresser; I need to get Chaos people over here to get rid of Lay and clean up.

I have already told Alicia everything, so she knows that I was going to get my son. I haven't told Nita yet, but she loves the kids and it will give her crazy ass somebody else's business to be in. As I look in the rearview mirror I'm reminded of why I have to make it out of this shit and bring Mayhem home to. I'm fucked up that it is nothing that I can do to get Ivy and Dijah home, but this is the game that we all choose. They got Ivy on the bodies he has caught alone and Dijah has been being followed and under surveillance for who knows how long.

~

Chaos went around back, and I kicked in the front door at Trice's spot. I need to get to him now and get some answers about these keys that I got from Ray. As I was walking through the living room Chaos was pushing Trice in my direction with the barrel of his gun pushed into his back.

"Nobody else is in here," Trice said, and Chaos left the room to finish checking the rest of the house.

"Look, I had no choice but to talk, and yo wife paid me too," Trice said.

"Muthafucka what?"

"Evelynn, came through here with her sister Monique and paid me to talk. If I didn't talk, she was going to have her pops people kill my momma and daughter man."

"What the fuck do these keys go to?"

This nigga talks too much and that's his fucking problem. The fact that Evelynn paid this nigga to testify against us doesn't surprise me. That bitch has done everything possible to try to bring me down. He gave me the address for the keys and I silenced him forever with a bullet.

Chaos has one bag filled with money and the other filled with guns poking out the top. "I'll get with you in the morning, I got to go handle something," I said as we went our separate ways.

My phone started ringing I figured it was Nita to want to discuss Amir. I can't give her a reason why Lay did what she did. It's Rossi, I don't want to answer because we don't have any business to discuss. When we were doing business, he made promises to always know what the fuck was going on at all times and shit his attempts to tell me his daughter wasn't shit; didn't prepare me for all the shit that's happening right the fuck now.

"Yea man, wassup?"

"I see that you're upset, but we need to talk. I have to go home, and I'll be back in a few days with something for Mayhem and you."

I agreed to meet up with Rossi. What I had to do is going to have to wait until I see Nita and the kids off in a few hours. Guadalupe agreed to go with Nita and the kids. Even though Nita swears she doesn't need her to go. With Harmony, Amir, Lil' M, Lil' Killa, Sharieffa, Lil' Steel and B. Her independent ass is going to need somebody until I can get there. The doctors and nurses are already in place to be able to care for Lil' M as long as he needs it. Nita doesn't want to leave here, but I think that she finally accepted the fact that she has to go.

I pulled into the driveway and Preston's car is in the driveway too. I ran in the house because it must be some more bullshit if he's at the house this early and didn't call first. I could hear Preston and Nita talking in the kitchen; well shit Nita is hollering.

Boom!

What the fuck is that? I knew that it's a fucking gunshot but who the fuck in here would be shooting a gun. I made my way to check on all the kids and all of them were still sleep. Nita is on my fucking heels and I got to Arie's room and pushed open the door I didn't see her. Nita went into the closet and I checked the bathroom.

"O my god M!" Nita screamed.

Arie is in her t-shirt and panties and the gun she used is lying next to her lifeless body. Nita is hollering and crying. I didn't see this shit coming and I know that she was going through shit from dealing with Mayhem, shit so am I, and he's my brother but killing myself isn't on my mind. I really got to get my family the fuck out here.

# SEVEN

## Nita

---

*I*'m trying to relax and not think about Arie, but I can't and the fact that B doesn't have his mom or dad anymore hurts me more than anything. Losing Ivy again is hell. I never thought that I would let him back into my life, but just when I do he is taken away from me again. I know that Messiah is going to fix everything, he always has. I just hope that everything that Mayhem has done doesn't make shit harder than it has to be. I've been holding this letter from Arie in my hand since I took it off her bed last night, but I don't know if I want to read it. I keep thinking that she did this because of something that has to do with Mayhem. I haven't told B yet and I'm not sure how I'll tell him either.

*I'm sorry for everything I wanted to tell you the truth, but I just didn't know how. I love y'all and Nita you have always been here for me and B. I would have loved to go with you guys and start a new life, but I can't go another day knowing that I was sleeping with a snitch. I started seeing Steel when I was with Loon and I only stopped because he went to prison. Since Steel has been out, I talked to him about all of the family business not knowing that he was working with the feds. I figured that since him and his brothers were so close he knew all the shit that had been happening not that he was going to turn around and use it against them.*

*Once I found out the truth I stopped talking to Steel and only saw him late last night when he threatened to kill me if I didn't come with him. I couldn't go with him. I should have never been fucking with him from the beginning. I can't go on knowing all the pain and hurt that I have caused this family knowing that I helped send Mayhem away. Mayhem did wrong and hurt me more than once, but it is killing me knowing what I have helped do to him and the rest of you. Please take care of my baby and make sure that he knows that I love him. I don't want to leave him, but I can't go on with this regret and pain that there is nothing that I can do to change. I know that you will take care of him and Messiah will show him how to be a man.*

*Love,*

*Arie.*

I wiped my face before one of the kids saw the tears falling from my eyes. If Arie wouldn't have killed herself one of us would have had to. I don't blame her, for what's happening I blame Steel for playing with Arie and bringing her into this shit. He knew more than enough to send us all away.

Mayhem is a muthafucka and he has caused so much bullshit, but he is my baby. I know that he has pushed Messiah to the edge more than once and I understand that. Getting on this plane is one of the hardest things that I have ever done but talking to Preston and him telling me that they were coming for me I had no other choice. Messiah is damn near out there all by himself and that shit is going to keep me up at night until he gets here.

I don't know how I feel about Alicia being back around. I mean she was cool back in the day but to just be around now got me questioning her motive too. I don't trust any fucking body anymore; all the shit that Evelynn did to us. While she was sitting in our face pretending to love Messiah and then to be working with his fucking enemies is something that I could feel was coming. You can't tell a nigga anything about his bitch even though I tried several times.

We are getting ready to land and I have to keep myself together to be able to make sure these kids are okay. Thank God for Guadalupe because with these bad ass kids by myself I had been done went fucking crazy. B, keeps asking me when his mom and dad are coming, and I just can't find the words to tell him just yet, but I know that I have to eventually.

# Mayhem

I looked over at my co-defendant's Khadijah and Ivy and back at Preston. He had better be getting ready to do a fucking magic trick and get us the fuck out of here. I just am waiting for them to bring their star witness in. I want to look at that bitch ass nigga. I would never have imagined that when I had him handling Trice baby momma Nikki who I had to tie up and torture for them to try to get them to let M go the night he decided to go to Lay's house. I would never have thought that nigga was working against me. That shit can't be right, I whispered and told Preston about that shit. How the fuck can a federal informant be getting away with committing murder while on the fucking job.

I wonder if Khadijah knew that this shit was about to happen, but shit if she did I couldn't see her not saving herself shit if for nothing else, so she could be there for her fucking kids. Being locked up makes me do nothing but think. I know that I don't have to question the fact that Ivy didn't know. He taught me everything that I know about the game and he for damn sure isn't working against me because if he was then he would be on the other side of the courtroom.

The courtroom got quiet, so I turned around to see what the

fuck had everybody's attention it was the man of the hour Steel's bitch ass. He had a Marshal in the front of him and another in the back. I see Chaos sitting in the corner wearing a suit and I see my young niggas Bull and Glock sitting behind me too. Shit even with them being here if they shoot up the fucking courtroom they'll be gone forever, and that ain't going to change what's going to happen for sure with none of us. I turned back around once the bitch was in front of me.

Melissa started with her questions first and this nigga couldn't even look in our direction. This nigga told everything that he thought that he knew. When the nigga started talking about shit that happened while he was gone I looked at Khadijah; she shook her head. I can't say anything bad about Khadijah and I never had to question her loyalty, but somebody fucking told her what was going on.

"Who was it that killed Nisha Sharief?" Melissa asked.

"Maurice."

"Do you see that person today in the courtroom if, so please point at him for the jury."

That nigga didn't hesitate to point at me I looked over at Khadijah and Ivy. Ivy was shaking his head and Khadijah was ready to kill that nigga, if only we could get a fucking gun. I would have risked it all and sealed my own fate without waiting for the fucking jury to decide. I need to do something and quick, or else I'll be in here for fucking ever and a day. I want to know where the fuck is M and why he isn't sitting here next to my black ass. This bitch Melissa wants him bad and we all know that. Fighting crime my ass! This bitch mad that she couldn't be that niggas fucking wife and that is the only reason we in this bitch now.

"Please explain to the jury how you know all of this considering you weren't there during the murder of Nisha," Melissa said while facing Steel and then turned and looked at me fucking smiling. "I know all this happened because of a relationship that I had with Arie."

"Please explain to the people of the jury who Arie is."

"Arie is Maurice's girlfriend. That I was also seeing before I got locked up."

I looked over at Dijah and I can tell by the expression on her face that she didn't know that Steel had been fucking Arie. It's nothing that Ivy or I can say that's going to make Khadijah feel better. With the shackles and handcuffs that they have us in if we wanted to get to that nigga, we wouldn't be able to do anything.

"You fucking rat ass bitch! I'm going to get you stupid muthafucka!" Khadijah screamed out jumping up from her seat.

"Mam. I'm going to ask you one more time to have a seat or you are going to have to be removed from the courtroom.

The Marshals stood up and came and stood by us. Damn, so Arie got with me knowing that she had been with my fucking brother. Steel kept talking about how he knows that everything that he was told by his lover Arie was correct.

"Object, hearsay your honor," Preston yelled out.

None of that shit fucking matters. The jury already heard it. Even though this nigga is the scum of the fucking earth and the fact that he would turn on us makes them twelve people looking at us decide if we did it or not.

"So, you talked to Khadijah and you know that she was going to be murdering Ezekiel?" Melissa asked, looking back at us.

"Yea, she told me she did—"

"You lying ass bitch I never told you that! You should have just taken yo muthafucking time. You fucking coward! You're a weak ass bitch! I fucking hate you lying ass bitch!" Khadijah screamed.

The Marshals snatched her up and took her ass out the courtroom. We could still hear her ass from the hallway. This pussy ass nigga can't even sit still in his seat. I know that Khadijah didn't tell him that shit. There is no reason why she would have needed to. That shit was on a need to know bases. Shit, the only reason why I know is that I needed to fucking know. Zeek was responsible for running me my money and him missing, shit I knew that my brother was trying to clean up my mess. His ass better be out there cleaning up now.

# Messiah

"Alicia, you can't just stay here by yo self and I got shit that I have to handle," I said as I'm getting dressed.

"Messiah, I'm not leaving and if you don't want me to stay here by myself then I'm going with you."

I don't want Alicia in this shit, but I don't have time to argue with her either. She's been trying to convince me that she is ready. I know that she ain't new to this; when I first started out she was right there with me through it all. I don't want her to get caught up in my shit. I got to go clean up some shit that Mayhem started on the block but couldn't finish. This shit could have been avoided, but I can't leave anything unfinished or it's just going to come back to me later.

I looked back, and Alicia was sitting on the edge of the bed with a gun on her lap. I couldn't help, but smile. Alicia has always been loyal and sweet, but I know that there is another side to her and niggas are going to see that side today. I leaned down and kissed her on her lips, I want to do more, but I got to handle this shit right now while I know these niggas are still in the same spot.

The good thing about Alicia is I don't have to give Alicia any fucking instructions she knows the game and knows how this goes.

Her dad and uncles wherein the game too so she was raised up in this shit just like me, so she knows the consequences and the benefits of this shit all too well. We jumped in my black Jaguar XJ and made my way down to The Palace.

It's almost opening time so the niggas that I need to get are the only people in there. Baby Zeek, G, and Rich were in there giving there cussing out the people. I'm sure for whatever Mayhem has cost them this month. Baby Zeek was doing the talking and the other bitch ass niggas are just cosigning. Without Baby Zeek, none of these niggas are able to eat. I know my brother, so I know he finessed his way into business with Baby Zeek too. I'm sure the nigga didn't have an option to take the dope and still kick out a percentage. The type of nigga Mayhem is I'm sure he was getting his cut and still having niggas run up in their spots and take more. I know my brother and he'll make a way out of no way to get you for all that he possibly can.

"That was a wonderful speech that you just gave real motivational, but all you muthafuckas need to back the fuck up," I said pointing towards the stage. The money makers Red and Foreva were used to this shit, they just threw their hands up dropped their bags, and made their way to the stage. I'm sure muthafuckas run up in here and rob them all the time. These new young and dumb bitches went to screaming and one by one Alicia, knocked them to the ground with the butt of her Glock.

I can't help but smile knowing that she's all mine and I don't have to question her loyalty because she's showing me that she's with me now more than ever before. Baby Zeek is just like his bitch ass daddy and he's good at playing gangsta until a real gangsta is in his face. Now suddenly, he doesn't have anything to say. Rich is my cousin, but he always been a bitch. Blood or not once you start fucking with the other side, you die too.

"Cuz, I'm working for Mayhem on this one I'm not really with these niggas," Rich said pulling out his gun and pointing it to Zeek's head," Rich said while laughing.

"Nigga you going to have to show me and you know that," I said between looking over at Alicia.

Bop! Bop! Rich hit Zeek and G both in the head making them both smack the floor face first. I know this nigga is probably working for Mayhem too that is the only way that he would be able to keep an eye on Baby Zeek for sure but, I don't trust him, so aunt Tina will be in a black dress soon. One of the young bitches couldn't handle seeing the sight of the boss and his main man laid out so she began to scream and holler bloody murder.

"Shut the fuck up bitch you are giving me a fucking headache!" Alicia screamed, grabbing the bitch by her head.

While the one bitch had stopped screaming and is now begging for her life; another bitch tried to make a run for it. Alicia shot her once in the back she stumbled, and I hit in her head and she tumbled over. I made my way up to the stage. Foreva has been doing this stripping shit forever. She is the one that is bringing in the money and her old ass needs to be preparing to retire.

"Yo old ass ain't ready to retire yet, girl?" I asked.

"Murda, it looks like I have no other choice now shit," Foreva said pointing at Baby Zeek and G.

"We can work something out, for the both of us," I said.

I heard a loud smack echo throughout the building and I know it was Alicia ass. I'm not offering this bitch no dick, but I'm sure that's what the fuck she heard. "Nigga don't play with me," Alicia said putting one hand on her hip.

"Chill, the fuck out this ain't that."

Rich was relaxed and too damn comfortable for me. He started smoking a blunt without a care in the world. "Come on nigga, I need yo ass to open the safe," I said making my way to the back. I know my crazy ass girl got them covered so I ain't worried about them doing nothing crazy. When we got to the back, he went right to the safe and opened it without too much talking which was fine by me. He called himself dividing the money into two piles. I don't give a fuck about that little money, but his ass was concentrating really hard trying to make sure that it was even. I just wanted the deed to the strip club and the rest of the paperwork.

"Here is yo cut, I just need to make sure me and mines is good.

Let Mayhem, know that I got him if he needs anything just let me know I got him and B," Rich said.

Bop! Bop! Bop!

I was thinking about letting him go until he told that lie that he had my brother. This nigga will be the same nigga if I would have let him live that wouldn't do shit for Mayhem but continue to eat off his fucking name. I made my way out to the stage, I let Foreva know that my people would be in touch and wrapped my arm around Alicia and we made our way out. There was no need to give any of them a lecture about not talking about what happened here the message has been sent.

∼

Alicia just fell asleep, so I could get out the house without her. Where I'm going, I didn't want here to be involved in this shit. Lady H had come through with the favor, so I could find out where Melissa's people lived. Lady H crazy ass suggested going to take out the jury and gave me the information to the hotel they were staying in. That ain't something I got the manpower to make work. All the niggas I got working for me I need on the block now more than ever. Even with Lady H people that are on her payroll being the ones watching them I couldn't risk doing that shit tonight.

When I was fucking on Melissa I was with Alicia, so I wasn't even bout to tell her nothing about this part. Everything has been going good, and the last thing on her mind should be and any other bitch. Since she found out about Melissa she wasn't going to want to hear anything about that shit.

Considering what's going on I know that they have her being watched by the feds. They can already just about imagine that she would be the muthafucka to get first. Getting to her would be wonderful, but I also know the heat that would come with that shit so right now she gets to live. I pulled up down the street from Melissa's mother Kendra's and made my way up the street to her house. I crept through the back door, so I could get what I needed from the kitchen and made my way to the front where was she was sitting watching the eleven-o clock news.

I shot her in the back of the head, so I could get to the shit. I needed Melissa to know that I wasn't playing sorry for her people but should have let the fact go that I would never be her nigga a long time ago. I could hear the shit was boiling in the kitchen. I took the meat cleaver and cut off all of Kendra frail fingers which didn't take much. I went to the kitchen to get the boiling water and poured it on to her body damn near instantly the blisters began to form all over her body. I needed to get her fucking head off and then I could be out.

My phone is beeping in my pocket, but whatever it is going to have to wait. I know that the kids are all good cuz I just talked to Nita. I finally got her head and threw into the bag and made my way to the next spot her sister Kay's. Kay doesn't live far away from their momma, so it didn't take me long. As I was making my way to the back door I was met by Alicia who was making her way out.

"I'm fucking helping, and I don't give a fuck what you got to say," Alicia said folding her arms over her chest.

"Girl bring yo ass, so we can get this shit done," I said slapping her ass and following in behind her.

# Alicia

All I been wanting forever is be back with Murda. I moved on with my life once I didn't see him ever coming back to me. It was only one nigga that I really fucked with who was Leek after Murda but after I ran into M at Killa's funeral nothing else mattered to me other than being by his side. I always knew that Evelynn didn't know what the fuck she had. I would never throw that shit into Messiah's face for choosing that hoe over me. I have him now and I'll never let him go to any other bitch ever again.

As we made our way around to take care of Melissa's people I felt safe and the throbbing feeling in my clit just made me even higher than I already am. Since I've been away from Messiah, my uncles have made sure I was good. I wasn't allowed to work; they too damn worried about something happening to me. My uncle C, is Ivy's best friend. Being in this business he made a lot of enemies and he thinks that I'll be the first to get touched. Leek was able to protect me, but he can't give me the feeling that I have from being with Messiah.

My uncle's girlfriend Auntee helped raise me and while uncle C and uncle Fifty were trying to keep me as far away from the game as possible Auntee had me all the way in the other side. I sent Auntee a text to go pick up my car, and she told me she was on it. This shit is in my blood and whatever I have to do to make sure that Messiah never leaves my side again will get done. No questions asked; shit is going to get done one way or another.

One after another we handled all of those closest to Melissa. Once we got to the last house, M looked at me as he put his car into park.

"What?"

"Nothing, you're fucking crazy. I love yo crazy ass doe," Murda said then kissing me.

"I got you when we get back to the spot, we got to finish this first doe," I said pulling back.

Finally, I got what I want and need in my life. I want to get that bitch Melissa, but I know it's a reason why M isn't trying to get her right now. I know that he thinks that I'm going to trip if he says anything about her, but I'm over that. When I was with Murda before I tripped about everything and he already knows that. If he didn't call me back within ten minutes I was popping up at the trap. I'm not on that shit and I know the minute I start back tripping about unnecessary shit we are not going to make it.

The last person left is Melissa's younger brother Devin he is the star quarterback for the Colorado Buffaloes. Luckily, he doesn't live in a dorm, I'm sure his big sister got him in this apartment so that he can focus on school and not partying, but from the looks of things around this muthafucka, the party is here. It's beer and liquor bottles all around and fucking coke. I'm sure her dumb ass is paying for that too.

I can hear shit falling and somebody crashing into shit coming from down the hall. M was making his way down the hall while I watched his back. M was signaling for me to move to another side of the hallway because this nigga must be in the bathroom. In perfect timing, I got out of his sight and he came stumbling out the bathroom. I knocked him to the ground which didn't take much since he fucked up already. M put him to sleep and we made our way back out.

"So, when we leave we can't ever come back?" I asked as M kept his eyes on the road.

"Is that going to be a problem?"

"I just don't understand why we have to leave. As long as we handle everything here we'll be good if we just stay here."

"Look, Alicia I'm trying to be done for good and there is nothing here for me anymore. I just need to know that you feel the same and that's something that you can handle."

I grabbed M's free hand, letting him know that I'm with him. The only thing is that I don't really want to leave my family. They mean everything to me and other than Messiah they are all that I have. I have to go and see my family later on, to let them know that I'm leaving. But right now, all I want is to give M all of me in exchange for all of him.

I damn near ran in the house to get cleaned up and get rid of these clothes. M wasn't far behind me. I heard a phone ringing, but it wasn't mine, so it must M's. We had to leave the hideout after Arie killed herself. I still can't believe that shit, but what's so crazy is that nobody knows why I never thought that she would do no shit like that. I love the new spot; I can't get too comfortable here because we are going to have to leave as soon as M finishes cleaning up behind Mayhem.

I started the shower so that I could push all bullshit to the back of mind and get ready for my man. I never thought that I would be here in this position again; it stills feel unreal. Everything that any woman would ever want is what Murda is. Yea he has his faults like everyone else and he isn't perfect, but he's damn near. I was nervous about being around his family especially Nita. She is cool, but I know how she feels about her sons and she doesn't mind cussing somebody out or fighting a bitch about her sons.

I jumped out the shower and got myself together and I'm not going to waste my time putting on no clothes because I want my man to see every part of me that he loves. M grabbed me from behind biting and licking his way down my back as he laid me on the bed, still kissing and biting me so hard, but it feels so damn. I perfectly arched my back and M began to eat my dripping box from the back. I'm gripping onto the sheets and attempting to get away from his grasp, but he isn't letting me get away. Just when I thought that he was done my legs were already shaking uncontrollably, but he just kept on going.

My mouth is dry, and he has sucked up all the juices in me. M slapped me on my ass and rammed his long, thick dick into my wet warm box. With every stroke M made I threw it right back. This nigga is beating my pussy from the back while tickling my clit. This niggas dick alone got me ready and willing to do whatever he needs me to do. He can get whatever the fuck he wants and however the fuck he wants it.

M rolled me over onto my back, not missing a beat still stroking my pussy like only he can do. I put my legs on Murda's shoulders and he went even deeper; deeper than he's ever been before. My legs began to shake again; fuck my whole body is trembling. M Leaned down and kissed me long hard and with every bit of him. After a few more minutes we both came together.

# EIGHT

# Mayhem

---

"*W*hat the fuck you mean she's dead?" I screamed passing around the small interview room.

"Maurice, I'm sorry, but you know considering what's going on your not able to talk to your family, so I had to be the one to tell you," Preston said, still whispering.

I know that Preston has nothing to do with Arie killing herself. I need to get the fuck out of here, so I can release some tension, and the only thing that is going to make me feel any better right now is to make some niggas bleed. Ivy is trying to take as much of the charges as he can. I don't want that, but he is, insisting on taking all the weight he can.

"I have some more bad, news."

"What the fuck else could be wrong?"

"This morning someone delivered Melissa's mothers head to her to the federal building."

"How the fuck could I have done that from in here?"

The way Preston is looking at me I know that they are trying to say that I did that shit too. All the shit that is going on I can't get my mind off Arie. How is B dealing with it? Was it something that I could have done to stop this? I just need to talk to Nita and get the fuck out here. I'm losing it right now; being locked up ain't shit, that ain't what's fucking with me. Not being able to be out there and handle shit that needs to be handled and be there for B that shit is killing me.

With the shit, with Melissa, that 's not going to do anything but postpone shit and make this shit drag out even longer. As I pace the room; I'm trying to think of what the fuck can I do and get it done fast. I leaned over the metal table and whispered to Preston a message that I needed him to get to M, so he could put it in motion to get me the fuck out of here.

"I'm working on trying to get a change of venue if we can get that there is a greater chance of you coming from under these charges," Preston said picking up his files and putting them in his briefcase.

"Whatever the fuck needs to be done make it happen. Whatever you need you got it, get me the fuck out here."

I knocked on the door for the guard to come and let me out. Preston better leave here and get to filling out whatever paperwork needs to be filled out, they need to take that bitch Melissa off the case and that will be one less issue that we fucking have. I made it back to my cell and grabbed my burner so that I can call Nita. I know why Nita didn't tell me about Arie, but I would have much rather heard it from her than fucking Preston.

I know that I've run my momma crazy and took her through hell over the years and I know that she is taking care of the kids while M handles the streets. As much as my momma and M keep talking this shit about leaving the streets and becoming a citizen that's not something that I'm ready to do. I'm going to be in the streets until the day I die. If I have to leave for a little while; I'm coming back. I can't leave the streets yet I'm not ready this is all I fucking know.

Nita answered on the first ring and confirmed that Arie had killed herself. "She didn't leave no fucking letter? What the fuck was going on with her, she didn't tell you anything?" I heard Nita, but no matter what she said, unless she told me that it was all a lie and Arie is in the other room it didn't matter. Nita assured me that M was getting shit together and holding court in the streets. It's not happening fast enough for me and my trigger finger is itching really bad.

"I told B about Arie's passing, but I couldn't tell him how yet."

"Let me talk to B."

～

"We have had to excuse, Ms. Brown from the case and Mr. Smith will be taking over," Judge Navarre said.

One less problem that I have to deal with; my snitching ass brother hasn't been ushered in here yet. Khadijah has been tapping her foot on the ground since they brought her in here. I don't put shit past anybody the devil once was a fucking angel, but I know that it's fucking with her hearing yo husband tell on you and then refuse to look in your direction.

"Can council, please approach the bench," Judge Navarre asked.

Preston and the new DA made their way up to the front. I wish they were just going to throw this shit out but that's not going to happen. I want to know where are the other fucking witness that they keep talking about I would love to see some of them. They have yet, to show they just keep pushing back their days for testimony and their star witness looks more terrified every time that he must come into the courtroom.

Preston came back over and whispered something to the other lawyers. The judge announced that he was going to lunch and we would resume in an hour. The Marshal that was taking me back to my cell pushed a piece of paper into my pocket.

# Evelynn

Fuck, I'm going to risk it all and run as soon as Moe leaves today. I can't take any more of this shit. I'll take my chances in the world alone another day here. Saadiya was cleaning up the house. We had just had our daily beatings, shit while I'm trying to recover she just goes on with her day. I'll be damned if I get used to some shit like this. The fact that she thinks that it's okay and acceptable for me to go through this shit with her is crazy.

I would never let my kids go through no shit like this. I just keep waiting for her to tell me that it is okay for me to run and that she will go with me, but it hasn't happened yet. How the fuck can you spend years in a house held fucking hostage and not one-time attempt to run. I'm not about to get brainwashed that this shit is normal.

"Your husband is in the front room to see you," Big Moe said in between laughing and then disappeared.

I jumped up and went to the front room to see what Messiah wanted. I knew from Big Moe that he was alive and not coming to save me as he beat me at my scheduled time this morning. I wish that right now he was coming here to say that he was coming to take me home, but that shit ain't going to happen. It is what it is, I did too much to take back. If he gave a fuck any more than he would have never let Rossi take me.

When I walked into the room he had a bitch was standing by his side. M looked different and fire that danced around in his eyes I have never seen before. Once I got up and got close to him and the bitch I noticed that it was Alicia. So, this is what this nigga does he goes back to his old bitch. I'm prettier than her, my ass is fatter than hers and I know my pussy is better than hers. As I looked down at what I'm wearing I started to feel insecure. I have never let a mutha-fucka see me sweat and I'm not going to start today. I don't give a fuck that this bitch is gucci'd down and I got on some dingy jogging pants and a shirt with a fucking hole in it. I ran my fingers through my hair and looked the bitch up and down and then at Messiah.

"What the fuck do you want?" I asked.

"Nothing from you, I just need you to sign here, here, here and there. Use the date that I did, back before you became a fugitive," Messiah said.

I snatched the papers out of his hand and Alicia's phone started ringing. She told whoever it was that she was with her man she would get back with them. I couldn't help but laugh even in my current predicament. As I flipped through the papers and glanced the wording; this nigga was not only trying to divorce me and leave me with nothing, but he also was trying to make me sign over the rights to my kids. I'm not legally giving away my kids. When I am able to get on my feet I'm going to get them. He is not about to play family with my kids and this bitch. They better go have a fucking baby.

"I'm not fucking signing this! Are you out of yo fucking mind?" I screamed.

"Alicia, give me a minute," Messiah said standing up.

The bitch moved across the room but didn't leave the room. She folded her arms across her chest. I don't give a fuck if the bitch heard every word that we had to say at this point it really doesn't matter. M made his way over to where I was sitting and stood in front of me.

"So, you're not just going to willing sign the papers?" M asked.

"No, anything else you fucking want?

"Get her and make sure she put, the right date so we can get this shit over with," M said kissed the bitch Alicia on the lips and made his way out the room.

I stood up and ran up to the bitch before she could do the same to me. I hit her a few times in the face and every time I hit her, she hit me with so much power that I was fighting to stay on my feet. With me not having as much energy as she has been damned near malnutrition she has me at a disadvantage. This would be a great time for my mother or fake ass sister to come in here and be some fucking assistance. Alicia, hit me so hard in my head that the room started to spin, and I fell back into the wall. She began to ram my head into the wall.

While I was attempting to loosen her grip on me I couldn't and with me not even being able to see straight, there is nothing that I can do to even make it out this one with a win. Alicia banged my head so hard against the wall that the windows in the room began to shake, then she grabbed me by my neck and slammed me to the ground. Got on top of me and began to beat me like I was fucking her husband and not the other way around.

# Alicia

When M told me to give him a minute, I wanted to jump on him and then beat the fuck out of Evelynn, but I didn't. I understand that this is something that needs to be done, but what I won't be doing is leaving the fucking room. He should have made the decision to do this when I wasn't fucking with him. When he told me to get her, shit that was music to my ears and what the fuck I wanted to hear from the moment we walked in here. I stopped hitting the bitch in her head before she blacked out and got off her and grabbed the papers and turned to the first page that she needed to sign.

I pulled out my Glock and put it to her head in case she still thought she wasn't about to sign it. She hesitated again, and I pulled out my Taser and shocked the fuck out of her. Rossi doesn't want her dead, is the only reason this bitch isn't dead because if I kill the bitch whether these papers get signed or not it wouldn't be fucking matter. M wants the papers signed and backdated so that Preston can go ahead and get them processed before we leave. The bitch got to signing the papers and I snatched them out of her hands and kicked her across the room. I made my way out to leave this bitch to rot in this fucking house. I'm still going to tell M about himself, asking me to leave the fucking room.

Alicia

~

M sent me to empty Ray's safety deposit boxes; while he handled something else. As I walked into the bank I started to feel uneasy, but I brushed it off. Shit, all that can happen is they won't let me get access to the box. The banker lets me right in without a problem. He handed me the boxes and I emptied the contents onto the table that was in the room. The banker just stood there watching, me. I looked at him crazy as fuck, so he finally made his way the fuck out the room.

M wanted to know if it was any paperwork one of the boxes pertaining whatever Ray told the feds. I went through the envelopes one by one and I found an envelope that had Uncle Fifty's name at the top. Something in me was saying that it was just a coincidence and it wasn't about him. I laid the paperwork down and went to the next envelope. I couldn't find anything that said Messiah or Mayhem's name or anybody else that mattered. I made my way through the other two boxes and as I put everything back I started to think what if the shit that I read was about my uncle Fifty.

I snatched the papers up and took them with me just in case. I made my way out the room and back into the bank's lobby. The security guard was staring at me that was sitting behind the security desk. The other security guard who is walking around making his rounds he also is looking at me. I got my ass up out the fucking bank; just in case something was about to go down it wouldn't be fucking today. I had to go and talk to Auntee and catch her up on what my plan is to leave with M.

I know that my uncles are not going to want me to leave. They don't have a problem with M; they really like M but them not being able to come across town and make sure that I'm good is not going to be something that they will just welcome with open arms. My mom died when I was a five, so I don't remember much about her. My dad died of an overdose two years ago. With my father struggling with his addiction my uncles stepped up to raise me.

Once I made it to Auntee's I had to finish reading the paperwork that I took just to make sure that the feeling I'm feeling is nothing. I read through the paperwork and tears began to fall from my eyes. I can't believe this shit my uncle had cooperated against Ray in exchange to receive a sentence reduction for killing my mom. All my life I have been told that my mother died from health complications and when my uncle went away a few years ago I was told it was a trafficking charge. How the fuck do you only serve seven years for murder.

I got my ass out the car and made my way into Auntee's and uncle C's. I know that if anybody would tell me the truth Auntee will, but what I want to know is why no one thought that this is something that I needed to know. I can't believe that Auntee and uncle C are okay with the fact that Fifty is a fucking informant. The thought that he was there, and has been there throughout my childhood, and he is the reason why I don't have my mom here is blowing me. He taught me how to ride a bike, taught me how to drive, and to find out now that he is the reason why I missed the years I did with my mom.

"Quiana, slam another door and I promise I'll break yo fucking hand!" Auntee screamed as I came through the front door.

"So, bitches get back with they old nigga and take out time from fucking and sucking to come see their family how nice of you," Auntee said.

I usually come over here all the time and since I've been back with Messiah I haven't been around much, but I always call her and uncle C. Even though I tried to stop crying before I came in here the tears just keep on falling. Auntee's back is turned to me so she hasn't noticed.

"Wassup Alicia?" Lil Sean said as he walked into the room.

Auntee is raising her nephew's kids; he and his wife were both killed so she stepped up to take the kids. It doesn't surprise me that Auntee decided to do that even though, she is crazy and will cuss you the fuck out. If she loves you she'll do anything for you without hesitation.

"Auntee, Alicia in here crying," Quiana screamed as she came out to snatch some papers off the table and then disappeared down the hallway.

"What is wrong with you Alicia? Did that nigga do something to you?"

"No," I managed to say while whipping tears away from my eyes as new tears fell to replace them.

I handed the papers that are soaked in my tears to Auntee and got up to go to the bathroom and get myself together. I must get to the bottom of this shit and I don't have too much time before we will be leaving. I can't leave until I handle this, so Messiah is going to have to understand.

I got myself together and made my way back into the living room and Auntee is on the phone now, "I don't give a fuck what you need to handle you need to get to this house right now, that shit is going to have to wait!" Auntee screamed, so loud that shit I jumped. I'm sure that she is talking to Uncle C; he doesn't take any shit from anybody, but I know that he'll be coming through the door real soon.

"I don't want you to think that I knew about any of this shit because I didn't and if this muthafucka did then we are going to have some fucking problems," Auntee said.

I knew that if anybody would be able to get to the bottom of this would be her. I don't have that much time if Uncle C knows anything he is going to tell Auntee before anybody, so I have a feeling that he doesn't know about this either. How the fuck this secret stayed buried for all these years is what I want to know. Why the fuck would he kill my mother? What could she had done to him and why have I been told that she died due to health complications instead of telling me that she was murdered.

"What the fuck is damn urgent that I needed to rush home now?" Uncle C asked as he rushed in the front door.

"Lil' Sean get out of here for a minute."

I handed the papers to Uncle C and as he began to read over them he sat down on the couch next to me. The look on his face told me that he didn't know anything about what the fuck uncle Fifty had going on behind his back.

"You think I knew about this shit?" Uncle C asked.

"So, what the fuck are you going to do about it? That's all that matters now," Auntee said, while she picked up Baby P who was reaching out to her.

"Alicia, you know that I love you and I'll do anything for you just like I'd do for my own kids don't you? You also know that I would never think that this type of shit is acceptable from anybody right?"

"Yea," I said.

I know uncle C and we have been close all my life, but I just don't understand how nobody knew that my mother was killed. I'm just starting to question a lot of shit. What else could be being withheld from me is there some other shit that I need to know.

"Alicia, I was told by your dad that your mother died due to issues with her heart. No, I wasn't going with Fifty to court when he caught that case, shit I can't. I'm going to handle this I'll be back," Uncle C said as he made his way back out.

I don't want him to handle it his way; I need to because that is the only thing that is going to help me with dealing with this shit. Auntee was looking at me like she wanted to say something, but she didn't know what to say. Honestly, there is nothing that she can say. The only person that can tell me anything is uncle Fifty.

"Auntee, I have to tell you something else."

"What?"

"I'm leaving town with Murda and I don't know when I'll be able to come back."

"I know how you feel about Murda but are you sure that shit is going to be different this time and that he is really done with that other bitch. If fucking not, I want you to know that I'm down to fucking ride out whenever."

"Auntee that's not an issue anymore; we are good I'm sure. He is persistent on being out the game and leaving, but I'm not sure that I want to leave you and Uncle C."

Auntee likes Messiah and always has, but I know that she had started to be close to Leek to. That's why is why I have been putting off telling her that I'm leaving. Just like I knew she would she bring up Leek and ask me about getting back with him. That's not going to happen I know that he is fucking hates me now, and that's cool with me I'm not tripping. He not going to get crazy or try no bull-shit because he knows what will come after that.

"I'm good on Leek. I'm where I want to be."

Auntee rolled her eyes and caught me up with everything that has been going on. My little sister lives with Auntee. Mya lived with me for a while, but we just couldn't get along. With her being sixteen she thinks she knows everything and we are just too damn much alike. She respects Auntee and she's scared of her, so she won't try the shit she was trying with me. She thought that she could come and go as she pleased in my house. Every other week she gets kicked out of school and she will not leave this bitch ass nigga named Bone along.

"Have you talked to Mya?" Auntee asked.

"Nope."

"She yo fucking sister and last time I checked y'all all that y'all got!"

The shit that I have running through my mind right now is way more important than my ungrateful ass sister. I busted my ass for her to make sure that she was good and no matter what I did for her it was never enough and she'd still turn around and be on some bullshit.

"You need to tell your sister that your leaving," Auntee said as she went to go and lay Baby P down.

Growing up seeing how Auntee held Uncle C down. She is going talk some shit and she doesn't play any games, but she was always there for Uncle C. He fucked up and it was some time that I just knew that she was done and was going to leave us both, but she didn't. The love that Uncle C has for her is something that I always watched and wanted somebody to love me the way he loved her.

Now that I finally have that type of love leaving here won't be that bad. I'm going to try to talk to Mya. Maybe I can talk her into leaving here and going with me. I didn't want her to stay with Auntee, but Auntee insisted because we kept getting into it. It's not Auntee's responsibility to raise Mya. Mya's mom can't even take care of herself so that's not an option.

"I'll call Mya later. I got to go handle some stuff and I'll call you later," I said as I got up to hug Auntee.

I still need to take care of some more shit before I go to the house. First things first I'm going to see if uncle C found Fifty.

# NINE

## Mayhem
_____

*a*s I put on the uniform that the officer gave me. I started thinking is this shit going to work or will I be caught before I make it to the fucking car. Fuck it! I'm going for this shit right the fuck now. M paid, off the guards to get me a uniform and to get me through the building and outside. Ivy been trying to take all the time and I'm not feeling that shit he feels like he needs to so that Messiah and I can be free to raise our kids.

I think that Khadijah is giving up and this shit is taking her under. When we go to court it's like she's in a daze can't focus and nothing seems to matter to her. M set up the same shit for her to get a uniform and to be ushered out of here with me, but she is persistent that she's not leaving just yet. I didn't need no convincing or talk about nothing shit all I needed to hear was that it was a plan in motion to get me the fuck out because the chances of me getting out of here sooner than twenty-five and up is real fucking slim.

Not to mention, it's some shit that I need to handle that Messiah not going to take care of the right way. It's some shit that you must handle on yo own if you want it handled the right way. I need to be able to go and see about Miracle and B asap.

As I walked with one CO in front of me and another behind

me, my trigger finger started to itch the closer I got to the door. I feel like the fucking CO in front of me is walking too damn slow for me. I wish that when I got out of here I was able to go home to Arie and my kids but isn't going to happen. I missed her funeral and the only thing that I will have is going to be the memories that we shared good and bad.

This shit worked, and the door is a few feet away. Once I got outside I looked around for a car that I recognized and couldn't find one and then I noticed a black Audi, A8 flashing their head lights. I made my way over to the car and M was driving. Shit, I'm damn near out of other people that it could be.

"You can drop me off to the first trap," I said, as I got in the car.

I need to be able to move how I move without somebody watching over my shoulder and if Nita and em ain't at that hideout there is no reason for me to be. I'll let him keep on being in love.

"I'm leaving on Monday at twelve midnight," M said.

"You not taking Alicia with you?"

"Yea she's coming."

I nodded my head. I guess that was his way of saying mutha-fucka if you're not there on time yo ass will be left. I don't want to leave but shit right now I don't have any other options. I got to get the fuck out of here to be able to stay fucking free. Staying here ain't gone do shit for me. Ain't shit else here for me, I got to go collect some money and clean up some shit but after that I'll be ready.

"I'll see you at the airport," I said as I got out of the car.

~

"Where the fuck is the money?" I screamed.

"I just need a few more days, just give me until next week," Rah tried to bargain with me.

Clearly, niggas think that they got forever. How long I have been gone it makes no sense for this nigga not to have my money ready to come to me. I pulled out my forty-five and shot Rah in the center of his right hand.

"Look, I just need a few more days pleaassse." Rah pleaded.

Nothing matters anymore. I 'm not letting anything go and I'll get some fucking sleep when I get on that plane in a week. I want all of mine I don't give a damn if it's a dime if it's mine I want it. I sent Reason to make his way through the house. Reason has been fucking with us for years, he runs one of my spots for me. I shot Rah in the leg, I need something to do to make the time go by, while I wait for Reason.

They thought that September 9, 2016, was something I'm going to set this bitch on fire before I leave here. Messiah's has been calling me, since shortly after he dropped me off. I'll talk to that nigga on the plane. I got my own ass to cover and my own shit to regulate. He is running around with that bitch Alicia like they are fucking Bonnie and Clyde; so, he can keep doing him and I'm going to do me.

"Muthafucka I'm waiting for you to tell me where everything else is," I said as I walked around the room losing my fucking patience.

My phone started vibrating, it's a message from Lady H; I'll be in at two tomorrow, we need to talk. So, I guess I'll have to talk to Messiah sooner than planned. Rah was starting to be for help. He must be fucking delusional, "Alright, tell me where that nigga Leek is at and I'll get you to the hospital."

Rah told me everything that I needed to know, and I silenced his bitch ass forever. Reason and I made our way out with the money that was owed to me and some. Reason is going to have to ride with me until it's time for me to leave. I'm sure that Messiah is setting shit up for Chaos, but I can't leave Chaos fucked up. It's about time that they meet so they can work together to keep shit going until I'm able to come back home.

I jumped in my car and Reason followed me. I need to call M and see where he is at. He didn't answer, but he sent me a text that said to meet him at our first trap. I switched lanes and made my way there. I know that this is going to be a muthafucking conversation. I want to see if Alicia is really, down M will see soon if he should have left that bitch where she been at. "Are you and yo brother good?" Reason asked as we pulled up to the trap. Shit I mean we alright, but if I said that I trusted him with my life I'd be lying. He paid, the guards to bring me out but shit he could be gunning for me after this week is up.

He doesn't agree with my tactics for handling business. Shit, it works for me; I got to where the fuck I'm at doing the same shit. It makes no sense for me to switch up now. I'm sure Messiah got a list of reasons why I need to change. I'm on the run and hot. Shit I been hot; so, he going to have to come up with something else. "Just, be ready just in case," I said, in between hitting my blunt.

When we walked in M was leaning against the wall that between the living room and dining room. Just when I thought that bitch Alicia wasn't here, she came from the back. I relit my blunt that had went out waiting for this nigga to get to it.

"Mayhem, damn do you understand that you just snuck out of a jail and the Marshals are running through shit trying to find you?" Messiah asked.

"Nigga what's new? I got shit to do, and if we are leaving in a week than I got a week to get it done. I need you to set up something with Chaos and Reason, so they can meet and get in position."

"Do you fucking understand if you get caught, I'm getting on the fucking plane without out yo ass!" Messiah said, walking towards me.

"This is business and ain't no honor amongst gangstas nigga you know that," I said, threw my blunt on the floor and stepped on it and made my way out.

I'll just make sure that Reason is nearby the meeting with Lady H since Messiah still acting like a bitch. I got other shit to do than talk to a nigga that think he my fucking daddy about all the wrong that I've done today. If he thinks that little shit was something, he better gets fucking ready.

# Messiah

I knew that Mayhem was going to get right into the streets instead of sticking to the plan to just lay low so we can get out of here but that is just too much to ask from him. Lady H wants something else, but I'm not sure what. I haven't told her yet that I'm out the game. I'm surprised that the feds haven't come for me yet, but I can feel that they are coming. Why Mayhem is going around trying to collect he'll soon see that a lot of them niggas have been laid to rest.

I have to cover my own ass at all costs. Mayhem is going to make shit even worse than it is. I have been running all the possibilities through my head of what could happen but until the shit happens it's nothing I can really do to prepare myself because Mayhem is back in the streets again. I promised Nita that I would get him out; so, I made that happen, but I don't know if I am going to be able to keep him alive.

"Are you okay?" Alicia asked me.

"Yea, I'm good.

We needed to make our way to one last spot hopefully before Mayhem. This nigga Chase has been doing all type of shit for Mayhem over the years. Mayhem doesn't know I know about him because I've never brought it up before. It was never any reason for me to care about it until now. I need to make sure that anybody that could be put into play against me is not able to and anybody that Mayhem was doing business with outside of our circle could become a fucking problem.

Mayhem the type of nigga he won't give you what he owes you. He'll spin you and have you putting in more work when he still owes you from the last time and that's why he always has so many fucking problems. It's not like he doesn't have the money to pay. Money has never been an issue for us. Mayhem is greedy, and nothing is never good enough for him.

Once we got in front of Chase's spot I killed the engine and Alicia jumped out wasting no time to get this shit done.

I know that she's dealing with the shit from finding out about her uncle and the truth about her mother's death. I told her she didn't need to come with me today, but she insisted. As soon as I hit the fob to lock the door Nita started calling she's going to have to wait because I know that she wants to know how everything is going. She trying to get back here, I keep telling her ass that she can't come back but every day she got a new reason why she can help.

I made my way through the front door, since it was unlocked, and Alicia was right behind me. Chase always comes here alone, so I don't expect for too many people to be here with him. When we walked into the living room it was like Chase knew I was coming and was just waiting for me. "I knew this shit was going to happen. I been loyal and stayed ten toes down for Mayhem and yo organization for years and this is the thanks I get?" Chase asked. That would be something that only Mayhem could answer I don't know why the fuck Mayhem fucked him over, what I do know from hearing him talk is that shit don't sit right with him and breathing too much longer can cause more bullshit to happen.

"I got it, Messiah," Alicia said as she leaned in to kiss me on the lips.

If I didn't let her handle the shit since she done asked without my assistance, I'll be having a conversation about the shit all night long. She can get this one, I made my way through the house to check the rooms and made my way outside so, that I can call Nita back.

# Alicia

"What the fuck are you doing with this nigga?" Chase asked, as soon as the door closed behind Messiah.

"We are back together. What the fuck are doing in business with Mayhem? Does Uncle C know this shit?"

My gun is pointed towards him and looking at my cousin in the eyes is just making me think about the shit that his dad Uncle Fifty has done that I haven't been able to find. Uncle C keeps trying to convince me that he is on it and everything is covered, but I won't be able to sleep until I know for sure that it is.

"Are you going to fucking kill me for a nigga? You're my fucking cousin!"

"And your dad is a fucking snitch. That killed my mom," I said as I let off several rounds into Chase's body.

Fuck Chase and Uncle Fifty and if nothing else won't bring Fifty out of hiding his son's death will. I didn't know we were going to get Chase, but when we pulled up I to the house, I was so damn eager to get inside hoping that Fifty was hiding out here. I made my way out to the car. Messiah was leaning against the car waiting for me. He opened the door for me and I got in checking my phone to see if

Auntee had called with an update, but she hasn't. I must go and tell Mya I'm leaving.

I told Messiah about what was going on with my family, but I don't want him to get involved. He has enough shit to worry about with Mayhem being back in the streets. I understand why Messiah got Mayhem out because he is his brother, but I don't understand why he continues to do business with him. Mayhem has caused so much bullshit and by the way that Messiah has been acting, he knows as well. He should have left him in there until the day it was time for us to leave. I don't trust Mayhem and I know that he is willing to do whatever it takes to get rid of Messiah and them being brothers isn't going to stop him.

I must be all the way together so that I can have Messiah's back, but until I handle my own issues I can't be at my best to be able to be of any assistance to Murda. Murda grabbed my hand and intertwined my fingers with his as he drove. The feeling that Murda gives me I don't want to lose again, and I now have more people that I have to look out for to make sure that we make it out of here together in one piece.

~

"Mya, I'm going to be leaving in a few days and I want you to come with me," I said while cutting my steak.

"I'm not leaving Bone, so I'm going to stay with Auntee and Uncle C," Mya said.

I knew that was coming sooner or later. I have tried to talk to Mya more times than I can count about why she needs to leave Bone alone. I remember how I was when I was her age when it came to Murda, so I know that it is nothing that anyone can tell her that is going to make her leave Bone alone until he leaves her. She has been dealing with him for almost a year and every other week she's crying about some shit that he has done.

"Mya, Bone is not the only nigga in the world. It's way better niggas out here that actually have something and can do something for you."

"I know you think that you the shit because Murda decided to come back around after he left you for another bitch, married the bitch and then that didn't work out, so he came running back to you."

I jumped across Auntee's table and onto Mya's ass. I'm sick of this ungrateful bitch. I could hear Auntee screaming telling me to get off Mya, but I don't plan on stopping. Fuck this bitch, she thinks that she can just say and do whatever she wants to and there is never any consequence for it. Auntee is trying to pry my hands from around Mya's neck. I'm on top of her choking the fuck out of her while banging her head on the dining room floor.

Uncle C picked me up and snatched me off Mya without a problem. "Girl, you kick me and you going to get the ass whopping you should have got a long time ago," Uncle C said as he took me out the room.

"Y'all, need to sit down and fucking talk. Y'all are fucking sisters, not enemies. Why y'all in here fighting each other. Did you tell Alicia that you're pregnant?" Auntee said.

I'm not surprised; I just didn't want this to happen either. Eventually, he'll be done with her and she'll be taking care of the baby by herself; depending on us to do what she is not able to. I could hear Mya crying in the other room, I don't know what the fuck she is crying for. That bitch started all this shit. I have done nothing but try to help her. I know what the fuck it's like not to have your mother around and with the lifestyle that our father lived when he was alive, he wasn't the most consistent or reliable.

"You ready to calm down and keep yo damn hands to yo self?" Uncle C asked.

"Yea."

I made my way to the dining room where Mya is still crying and Auntee is rubbing her back and comforting her. I rolled my eyes as I sat down across the table from them. "Neither one y'all better not break nothing in my fucking house. Alicia before you leave we need to talk," Uncle C said on his way out the room.

"Y'all need to learn how to fucking talk to each other. It's plenty of muthafuckas that's already against y'all!" Auntee screamed.

"I'm sorry. You just don't understand or care about what I'm going through. All you care about is yo self. You don't really care about me," Mya said in between her tears.

"I do fuck—" I attempted to say before Auntee cut me off.

"Did you hear what the fuck she just said. You need to learn how to talk to people, this ain't no shit in the streets this is yo damn sister!" Auntee said as she got up to leave the room; one of the kids are calling her name.

"Look Mya, I can't understand if you don't tell me what is going on. If you don't tell me how am I supposed to know?"

As Mya began to tell me what has been going on between her and Bone. There is nothing I can say that is going to change the things that she is going through or has been through. I wanted to keep her away from all of this and for her to never go through any of this shit with no nigga. Not only is she pregnant, but so is some other girl by Bone.

I walked around to her side and pulled her hugged her and just listened to her. I can't make her go and I know that she is not going to leave Bone alone until she is ready all I can do is be here for her. I don't want to leave her and then now to know that she is pregnant here. I have to just make sure that she knows that I am here and when she is ready her and the baby can come to me.

I sat with Mya for a few hours, I let her know that I would be back by before I left town. We both agreed to work on our relationship. I want us to be able to be close; Auntee tells me every time we talk that we are all that we have. I know how important family is to her and she has told me that ever since I can remember. I need to go and talk to uncle C, but I had finally got some help with finding Fifty via text message, so we'll have to talk another time. I made my way out the house and jumped in my car and made my way to talk to Uncle Fifty.

I jumped on the highway, so I can get to him before he fucking leaves. He was seen going into one of his bitch's house by my girl Dee Dee. I finally made my way to the house and as I popped the trunk to get my Glock out of my bag I checked my surrounding making sure I didn't see the fucking police around. If this nigga telling they could be watching him right now. All the cars outside of these houses are the people who live in these houses cars. Fifty have been fucking with Dee Dee forever and she has lived in this house all my damn life.

I made my way into the house, I knocked on the door and Dee Dee opened it and let me in. I hugged and greeted her like I do every time I see her. Then I head-butted her and put a bullet in her head. Dee Dee never did anything to me, but her nigga did. They have been fucking with each other for over twenty years and aren't married. They don't have any kids together, but he has plenty around the town with other bitches.

Fifty came running to the front room, and I shot him in the leg which caused him to fall to his knees. The bigger a nigga is, the harder they fall! He taught me that. Fifty is a big nigga and all my life I didn't think he could do any wrong. Uncle C and Fifty were like fucking Superman to me and couldn't do any wrong. If any wrong ever came close to me I knew that they would make shit right and shut shit down.

"Wait, wait. I can explain," Fifty said.

He had my fucking attention, I cleared my schedule just for him. I'm not leaving, and he isn't dying until he tells me what the fuck I want to know. I squatted down, so I would be eye to eye with him, so I wouldn't miss anything.

"I'm waiting."

"You were a kid, you wouldn't have understood what was going on that's why I never told you what really happened to your mom."

"Try me."

"You mom was responsible for making pickups for us and I started watching her closely. Not only was stealing from us, but she was getting high too."

If she was stealing money, why not just stop fucking with her involving business. Why kill her and why not tell me the fucking truth why do I have to accidentally find out? I have so many questions, but to be honest I don't think that it is going to make a big difference in my life if I know. The only reason why he admitted to the shit is to save his own ass from more time in the feds. I shot Fifty in his other leg just to see if it was something else that he needed me to tell me. I'm not sure if I believe his excuse or if he is just not telling the whole story.

"Okay, okay. I was in love with your mother and she wouldn't leave my brother for me."

Soon as the last words left Fifty's mouth I put two bullets into the center of his forehead. I wanted to know the reason why and I got it, why he decided to tell on somebody else is not business, and where he is going he won't be able to tell on anyone else. I made my way out to my car and even though I thought silencing uncle Fifty was going to make me feel better and everything in my life would go back to normal, it's not. One of the only people I have ever been able to trust and depend on has been by my side I just had to kill. I wiped away the tears that are attempting to fall from my eyes and made my way home to Murda.

# TEN

# Messiah

---

*a*s we sat around a conference table in the Four Seasons Mayhem and I have barely said two words to each other. I just wanted to get the fuck out of here, so I can get back to handling the shit that I need to with my legal affairs.

"Glad to see that your home," Lady H said.

"Shit, I'm glad to be home," Mayhem said.

"Alright, well I wanted to meet with the two of you because I need to handle some things and since none of my family is capable now to step up and take over temporarily. I need to know if the two of you would be able to?"

Mayhem's eyes lit up like he had been wanting to hear those words all his life. I think he just ignored the fact that she said this is temporary. She has three sons and when they're ready to take over that will be who is in control of the business. All Mayhem heard was take over. Mayhem wouldn't be able to handle that type of power. He can't handle the fucking power that he has now.

"I know it's a lot to think about and I know that you need some time. Not a problem; I completely understand. I also have something as an incentive; I can make sure that both of your charges disappear," Lady Heroin said.

"Were in," Mayhem said.

"We are going to have to get back with you Lady H. I need some time to think about a few things before I can make this type of decision," I said while staring at Mayhem.

He knows damn well that I'm getting in position to be out of the game for good. So being a temp for Lady H, isn't going to fucking work for me. Mayhem thinks that he is fucking made of Teflon and is fucking unstoppable. This nigga already thinks that he the fucking plug, so that type of notoriety isn't going to do Mayhem any good. The charges disappearing sound fucking wonderful but taking on all her problems on top of our that shit is something that I'm not ready for. If Mayhem would just be real with himself, he isn't ready either.

"Just let me know when you two are able to make a decision. You will forever be connected at ten a key. I'll always be able to make sure that you both are protected from law enforcement," Lady Heroin said.

Lady Heroin's men opened the door from the outside and she made her way out the room. "What the fuck? Are you dumb nigga, did you hear what she said?" Mayhem screamed hitting the table. I just looked at this nigga. We got the same mom and dad and were raised under the same roof all of our lives, but this nigga just doesn't get it.

"What the fuck? Don't you understand that I'm not trying to do this shit forever, don't you understand? Nigga, look at this shit ain't no forever shit. I'm all that my fucking kids got, and I can't be there for them from the feds!"

"Nigga she just said that we won't have to worry about the fucking law! Nigga, I need this shit! This is all I know! This is all I got!"

"Muthafucka what about the cops and the feds that ain't on her fucking payroll? Nigga then do this shit, but when I get on the plane I'm done! I'm not coming back here. What the fuck are you doing this shit for, the money or the fame cuz nigga you got just as much money as me! You could be doing some other shit by now!"

Mayhem stormed out the room. I'm sick of this nigga and his bullshit. He wants to run shit but can't he doesn't know how to. My phone is vibrating in my pocket; I checked it and it's Nita. I can't worry about Mayhem right now, I got to go get some shit in place with Chaos. Chaos is going to be taking over. I know that Mayhem wants to, but that isn't possible. Before I go see Chaos I made my way up to Lady H's room, so we could finish our meeting. I met with her earlier, so I already knew she wanted us to work, to take over for her. I know she is used to me always riding with my brother right and wrong, but Mayhem is not willing to handle business on my terms, so this shit will never work.

I just have to make sure that Chaos is going to be good. Lady H wouldn't work with just one of us before, but I need to make sure that Chaos is still able to keep our territory. Even though I want to be done with the game I can't lie, for a long time this street shit was all I knew too, but I always knew that I had to make other arrangements because I can't do this forever.

I knocked on Lady H's door and the door swung open. I just need to make sure that she is able to still supply Chaos. Chaos has stood tall and he is damn near all that have out here. He isn't ready to leave the game yet and I understand that you have to go through some shit and be ready to leave it alone.

"Look, you want to be out the game, I'll have to respect that. I just need one more thing and I'll make sure that Chaos is able to continue to eat. I can also get the feds to back up. You and Mayhem for sure and moms, but Ivy took a plea. I can see what I can do for Khadijah too, but we don't know what the fuck she done told her husband," Lady Heroin said, as she poured her juice over ice.

She always says that she never has drunk liquor or done any drugs, and she doesn't need to. She can get crazy without it. That shit is for sure true! I was all ears to whatever I needed to do. She wanted me to kill some nigga named JT. He owes her money and has yet to pay up. She gets real particular when she wants a nigga dead. She wants it done a certain way and at a certain time. I took in everything that she was telling me. When Lady H wants a muthafucka dead whoever is in the house has to die. If they are home with their bitch and kids, then they have to go too.

"If you change yo mind and want to come back into the business, your welcome back anytime. I'm considering offering it to Mayhem on his own."

"I'll be in contact once that is handled."

I'll never talk down on Mayhem to nobody outside of my immediate family. I'll never step on his toes in an attempt to stop Lady H from doing business with him. If she wants to do business with him, then that will be on her to clean up behind him and to be able to still run her business after he fucks up doing bullshit. When I get on the plane I'm done. Getting rid of this nigga is going to ensure that Chaos is good and then I can sit back and relax until it's time for me to leave. I have a meeting with Foreva and Preston about a business deal in the morning. I'll be able to get this nigga JT after that. I made my way out the hotel and to my car. One less thing I had to worry about now is the feds coming to get me. I can relax a little and breathe easier. My phone started ringing, it's Mayhem.

"Wassup?"

"I need you to go with me to handle something," Mayhem said in between choking on his blunt.

"Meet me at the house off Liverpool," I said and hung up.

I started to think about what the fuck it could be that Mayhem wants me to go with him for. Could this be a set up to just get rid of my ass? Just to be able to stay in business with Lady H. He stays on some hot shit, so the possibilities are fucking endless. This I owe him for September 9th shit is getting old. If I don't agree to go with him that's what the fuck he'll be bringing up that up.

# Evelynn

Syke has been here for a few hours, so now is the best time. Syke came through the front door and walked down the hallway to the bathroom. I didn't have shit here that I needed. I made a run for the door as soon as I heard the bathroom door lock. I could hear my so-called mother screaming "Them dumb bitches trying to run!" I looked back and Trina is right the fuck behind me. I ran as fast as I ever ran in my fucking life. I can't take another day there. They are not about to catch me. If they catch this bitch Trina that's on her; I don't plan on stopping until I get as far away as possible.

I see a cab, parked in the gas station parking lot a few blocks up. I'm surprised to see a damn cab; shit with uber and lyft I'm surprised they still in business. I made my way up to the gas station and Trina managed to catch up. The cab driver is getting in his cab, "Could you please give me a ride downtown," I managed to spit out while trying to catch my breath.

"No, I have a customer waiting for me right now," The African said.

"Please, I'll give you a thousand dollars. Please, I need a ride right now I can't wait.

I jumped in the back of his car and Trina followed. I see some cars coming up the street and they could be Syke. I ducked down and cab driver jumped in ready to get his money. I'm headed to the bank to empty the safety deposit boxes if Messiah hasn't got to them yet. Right now, all I can do is pray that he hasn't. The cab driver was willing to get a ticket for this money. I just keep on thinking about what if it's empty. Fuck this nigga! What the fuck am I going to do if it's empty.

We finally made it downtown and the bank is coming up on the next block. "Do you think that they will find us?" Trina asked. I didn't answer her because nobody told her to fucking come. Every time she tried to have a conversation with me; I cut her ass right off. "Stop right up here on the left. I need to run in the bank and I'll be right back," I said as he pulled over. I snatched the necklace off Trina's neck and gave it to the cab driver and we both got out. I look like shit and the faces of the people as we walked into the bank just made me remember.

Luckily as I scanned the lobby, Messiah's banker Karen noticed me. "Mrs. Jones. How are you? I haven't seen you in a while," Karen said as she looked at me like she was disgusted by my appearance.

"I'm doing just fine, just had to come run to the bank and get something important out of the safety deposit boxes," I said, and Karen lead me and Trina to the boxes.

I exhaled; I'm so fucking relieved to see Karen. I signed my name; used my hand and was let into a room. Karen excused herself why she went to get the boxes. I was relieved that she didn't ask for identification. If so I was going to be fucked. She brought the boxes in and excused herself back out the room. I opened the boxes one by one and they are still filled with cash and Harmony's jewelry and bonds.

I took all the money and jewelry and hauled ass out the bank. I don't know where the fuck Trina thinks she's going, but I'll give her a few dollars and she can get the fuck on! Once I got to the main lobby I started to feel uncomfortable and a sharp pain hit me hard in my stomach.

"Freeze!" Put your hands up!" An officer screamed once I hit the sidewalk.

I looked around and I was surrounded by police. The people that were downtown were just staring at me, shaking their heads and pulling out their phones to record me. I looked around again and I see Messiah walking up with Alicia, trying to get through the crowd to get in the bank.

"We are not going to tell you again, put your hands up now Mrs. Jones!" Another officer screamed.

They must be looking for me for momma Janice's death. I thought that shit would be in my rearview mirror until I walked out of this bank. I looked over at Messiah again and he didn't have a care in the world. He actually looked happy with another bitch.

"Get him! He's the one you're looking for he is wanted for murdering, drug dealing and some more shit! Get him!" I screamed as some of the officers started to look in the direction I was pointing in, I tried to make a run for it. "Move out of the way!" an officer screamed over a blow horn. The people watching moved the fuck out of my way clearing a path just when I thought that I was going to get away. I couldn't look back I had to at least try to get away. Going to prison isn't a fucking option that I have.

Rat, a, tat, tat ringed out and one by one the bullets tore through my body and I fell face first on the ground. I don't have any more fight left in me; I just have to accept the fact that I fucked up. I can just see my life flashing before my eyes when shit was good, and I should have just been grateful I wasn't so this is the price that I have to pay.

# Messiah

As I watched the police gun down Evelynn in broad daylight; I didn't feel anything. I'm glad they did it. That means that I don't have to ever worry about her coming back. They won't let anybody in the bank, so I made my way to the courthouse. Alicia and I know that shit in Evelynn's hand is out of the safety deposit box, but it is what it is. I just got to take that shit as a loss. We made our way around the corner to the courthouse, so I can see for myself with my own eyes Steel.

Lady H did like she promised and made Mayhem, Nita's and my charges go away. I handled JT and we are even. She still wants us to take over, but I'm slowly cutting all ties with Mayhem. I won't be mad if he doesn't show up at the airport tomorrow. I haven't heard from him, but I watched the news and I know he is responsible for more than half the shit I saw on the news this morning. I'm out the game, I made some money and I'm set for life there is no need for me to be in anymore.

We finally made it to the courtroom where Khadijah is at. I opened the door and Alicia went in first. Everybody in the courtroom turned around looking at us I nodded to Khadijah and sat down. Steel was on the stand talking Khadijah, whispered something to one of the guards by her and she stood up. Once she got in the aisle, one of the fucking guards handing her a pistol. It happened so fast I almost missed it.

Bop! Bop! Bop!

Rat, a tat tat tat.

All the people in the courtroom were screaming and the officers were rushing Khadijah. Steel was dead with the first shot. I grabbed Alicia and got the fuck out of the courtroom. Knocking over the other muthafuckas that were trying to get out too, shit now it's really done. Khadijah was probably never coming home, but she won't for sure now.

We finally made it outside and to where the car is parked. Alicia has to go say goodbye to her family. I told her I would come with her so I'm going. As I drove off Nita was calling. It's like she always knows when shit has gone from bad to worse.

"Yea momma," I said as the call connected to the car.

"It's over now," She said I could hear her exhaling through the phone.

"Yup, it's over."

# Alicia

---

I don't know what to say. When we walked into the courtroom I never imagined any shit like that to happen. I don't know how the fuck I would feel if my husband had testified against me. Shit has been happening so fast ever since I got back with Messiah; it's damn near a blur. I sat back and relaxed as Messiah made his way to Auntee's. Mya still won't come with me, but we have been working on our relationship. All I can do at this point is trying to be there for her and the baby as much as I can from where we are going.

Messiah still hasn't told me where we are going. Shit, I want to know; I gave up asking. Shit tomorrow will be here soon enough, and I'll see. As we pulled up to Auntee's and Uncle C's Messiah finished up talking to Nita and we got out the car. I still don't know how I feel about leaving. When I went to open the screen door; Leek was coming out the door. I moved out the way so that he could get by and made my way in the house.

Uncle C refused to go to Fifty's funeral. I'm trying to push that as far back in my memory as I can, but I think about that shit all the time. I never told Uncle C that I killed him, and he never asked. We haven't said anything about him to each other. Uncle C and

Messiah shook up. I left them to talk and went through the house to find Auntee.

"So, bitch you coming to tell us bye?" Auntee said as I walked in the kitchen.

I didn't say anything, I just sat down on one of the bar stools. Mya came into the kitchen; we spoke to each other and she sat down next to me. "I don't want you to leave," Mya said. I hugged her because it's nothing that I can say, I'm still leaving. I know that she will be fine with Auntee; I still wish she would just fucking come with me. Auntee walked out the kitchen and I could hear her talking shit and threatening Messiah. She meant that shit doe; I hope she doesn't fucking run him off.

Seeing Leek put me in a bad head space my phone started vibrating and it's a message from Leek, **you can still just come back home. Whenever you are ready; I still love you.** I put my phone back in my bag. That will never happen; if Messiah leaves me tomorrow. I wouldn't go back to Leek. I tried to talk Mya into coming with me again, but she wasn't having it, so I left it alone.

I'm sure that Auntee is getting on Messiah's nerves so I went into the living room to check on him. We sat and talked to them for a little while longer and I needed to leave now or shit I'm not going to ever leave.

"Take care of my fucking baby! Or I'll fuck some shit up! You think yo brother crazy you haven't seen crazy yet nigga!" Auntee said as she hugged me tight as hell.

I hugged all the kids and Mya and last was Uncle C. "You'll be good; we ain't going anywhere. We are gone always be here!" Uncle C said as he hugged me. Mya walked with us out to the car. She hugged me tight and I could feel her tears against my cheeks falling. I wiped them away and promised her that she can call me anytime, day or night and I'm going to be here for her and the baby as I rubbed her stomach. Auntee came and grabbed Mya from the curb and I got into the car.

Messiah grabbed my hand and kissed it. At least with the charges being dismissed; I can still come back and see them. That doesn't make this any easier for me right now. I know that Messiah has me now and he'll do whatever it takes to make sure that I'm good in every way. I love Messiah more than I have ever loved anybody.

When we pulled up to the house there was a car in the driveway. I looked at Messiah and he was just as confused as me. I pulled out my gun and he did too as we got out the car. A woman was sitting in the car. Messiah went ahead of me walking up on the car.

"Why are you here? You are supposed to be with the kids," Mayhem said as I put my gun away.

"First of all, you can't tell me where the fuck I can and can't go. If she let you tell her that's on her. I'm here because I'm no longer a fucking fugitive and I can be!" Nita screamed.

I made my way into the house and they were right behind me. I always have loved the relationship that Messiah has with his mom. She'll ride for them to the end and she doesn't give a fuck she'll get in the field right the fuck with them.

"Mayhem, is responsible for all this shit that's going on in the streets I been hearing about?" Nita asked.

"The four niggas that got dropped last night and the nigga and bitch that got shot the fuck up in McDonald's parking lot for sure. I don't know about that other shit," Messiah said.

"I'm going to handle it," Nita said.

Messiah didn't say anything. I know that Nita has always babied Mayhem and been right with him even when he on bullshit, so I don't know how the fuck she's going to handle him. Mayhem loves this shit. He loves seeing shit on the news that he knows he did. He came from under those charges, so he really thinks he is fucking invincible now. Messiah gave up on caring about what Mayhem does. I haven't even seen Mayhem around and I don't think that Messiah has even talked to him.

# Mayhem

I talked to Lady H and we agreed that we can do business with each other leaving M out of it. Now that all the dust has settled, I still need to even the score with my brother. My life has turned to shit. We had just got to a point where I didn't want to choke her to death and I get locked up and she kills herself. That's some shit that I don't think that I will ever get over.

The shit that I been doing the past few days I have been trying to make myself feel better to get back to my regular self. None of that shit has helped me; I'm going tomorrow to get B and Miracle and bringing him back home. I grabbed a black Nike jogging suit out my closet and threw it on. This nigga can't just go on with his life with his old bitch meanwhile fuck me and what the fuck is important. Neither one of my brothers ain't shit.

As I made my way downstairs I can hear somebody knocking on the door. I don't know who the fuck it nobody could be, but my momma even knows where I'm staying. I swung open the door and it's Nita. "What are you doing here?" I asked, as Nita pushed past me and way her way into the house. She didn't answer me, she just flopped down on the couch.

"Mayhem why damn? Why the fuck would you do this shit!" Nita screamed with tears coming down her eyes.

"What the fuck did I do now?" I asked.

Nita grabbed some tissue out her purse and blew her nose. Still not answering my question; I haven't done shit that would affect her precious son yet. I'm killing that nigga as soon as Nita leaves here.

"While Messiah, was out here trying to get you out. You were sending niggas money to make shit worse out here for M, so he would fall. The niggas that M and Lynn took out you paid them to be on that block. You paid Smoothe to steal money just, so M would lose somebody else too. The night when Messiah went in the club and took care of Baby Zeek and them you had paid them niggas to kill him too didn't you? Did you blow up Chaos house today? Good thing he doesn't live there anymore!" Nita screamed, while still crying.

The look in my momma's eyes I have never seen before. I was still trying to get that nigga knocked off, but it had to done in a method that I have never had to use before. I never told anybody that shit so how my momma knows I don't know. Nita stood up, from the couch so I figured she was leaving, she pulled out a gun and shot me in the chest.

"I did everything that I could do for you. I always stand up for you right or wrong and you turn around and try the same shit again! What if Messiah couldn't get the charges to disappear? Fuck me too hun? Did you forget they were looking for me too!" Nita screamed as she shot me again this time in my arm.

"Momma," I Managed to say, while coughing up blood.

She let off all the bullets she had in her gun and everything went black.

# Nita

That was the hardest shit that I ever had to do, but it needed to be done. I helped to create Mayhem. For years I made him think that the shit he did was okay because somebody was always there to bail him out. I'll always blame myself for allowing this shit to continue. If one of them niggas would have killed Messiah everything would have fallen apart. Messiah has always been the glue that kept shit together. Mayhem was selfish and didn't care about anybody but himself.

The only thing I feel bad about is the fact that B now has nobody, but us. Shit and Miracle too. Mayhem had to go. I know him and the look in his eyes he was headed to try to kill Messiah. I love Mayhem, but the pain that he has caused me and the rest of this family. I needed to be the one to handle this and now we can all go on with our lives. I originally just came back so that I can go see Ivy in the morning, but this was on my heart as well.

I pulled out Messiah's burner I took from the house and called Chaos, to come and clean up. I need to get the fuck away from this house, but I can't bring myself to pull off from the curb. I made my way back to Messiah's, so I can try to get some sleep. I tried to stop crying, so I don't go in the house crying, but the tears just keep on falling.

When I finally made it to Messiah's I gave up on stopping the tears and just went in the house. Messiah met me at the door and stopped me from hitting the ground. I'm sure that Chaos has been here and told him what I did. He didn't say anything and I'm glad because right now I don't want to talk I just want to see Ivy in the morning and get the fuck out of here.

# Messiah

I still can't believe that Nita killed Mayhem, but after she calmed down and ran everything down to me I know why she did it. I held her until she fell asleep and I took my ass to sleep too. That was the most peaceful sleep that I have ever had in my life. I'll feel even better when I get to my kids.

When I woke up Nita was gone, and Alicia was finishing up packing. I made my way out to ride through the hood one last time before we got to head out to the airport. Chaos still has shit running smoothly and I ain't worried about him he knows the consequences of this game. The feeling that I'm feeling I haven't felt in a long time I'm happy. I don't have to look over my shoulder and worry about nobody coming; trying to take anything from me. I got the girl that I was supposed to be with from the beginning, my kids Lil' M, Amir and Harmony. I finished turning corner and went to pick up Alicia, so we can leave. Nita is going to meet us at the airport.

When I made it to the house Alicia was waiting for me with all her bags. I put them in the car and we made our way to DIA. We are going to the British Virgin Islands. I know that Alicia is going to love it. She stopped asking where we are going. We made it to the jet and Nita were already aboard waiting for us.

Unlike many I was able to make it out. The shit wasn't easy, and it was some days that I wish I could take back, but shit what's done is done. I learned a lot of shit. Mayhem did teach me not to trust a fucking soul and that sometimes it is necessary to handle shit yo self. Never get too comfortable because shit can change every day. The pilot, announced we are getting ready to take off.

"I love you, Messiah," Alicia said.

"I love you too baby."

The End...

# SNEAK PEAK TO A EAST SIDE GANGSTA CHOSE ME TWO...

# Kurupt

---

*a*s I sit here waiting for Enforcer to get back from dropping off the money in the tunnel. I'm losing my fucking mind and Mina keeps calling me every five minutes. Now my momma is calling.

"Yea momma," I said as the call connected.

"I just called to check on you," Alice said.

I haven't been able to think about nothing about Hope. The fact that this bitch Quita would take her and then want a fucking ransom. If anything is wrong with my baby I'm going to kill that bitch's whole family. As I sit in the spot waiting for Enforcer to come back this damn front door is opening too many fucking times and E, still ain't back.

"Everybody that don't need to be here get the fuck out! Naw fuck that everybody get the fuck out!" I screamed

Everybody made their way out the door. I know that my momma is concerned, but she not helping either. I got her off the phone; I need to fucking think. E, finally walked through the front door and Gotti came in behind him. I had sent Gotti to see if what he could find out while I wait for E, to get back.

My phone started ringing and it is a private number so, I know that it's the call that I'm waiting for. I answered the phone and whoever the fuck it is Quita or soon to be dead ass nigga aren't saying anything. I'm screaming into the phone saying hello and nobody ain't saying shit and then they just fucking hung up.

"What happened?" Gotti asked.

"Not shit, they not saying nothing," I said.

The phone started ringing again. I took a deep breath as I answered the phone and putting it on speaker phone. I never imagined that I would be going through no shit like this. When Quita left, I did what the fuck I had to do for her and this shit is really fucking with me. Right now, I have to stay strong and do what I have to do to make sure that Hope come home.

"Bitch, where the fuck is my baby," I spit.

"How are you doing baby momma? I'm sorry I have been playing house with our baby with another bitch. That's how the fuck you should be talking to me," Quita said laughing.

"Quita you got the money; just tell me where my baby is at," I said trying not to go off while she has my baby.

"Enforcer I lover Envii's new Lexus. It's real cute. So, K get me one and then I guess you can have your daughter back. We'll have to see maybe or maybe not," Quita said.

I know Quita and I know how scandalous she is and I know the type of shit that she used to do. For her to be doing this shit and using my baby to get it is making me lose it. I handed E, the phone and walked out the house to get some air before I go off and that bitch does some more fucked up shit.

I grabbed my burner out the armrest of my car and called Bad News. I need to get some more people in the streets to see what the fuck is going on and Bad News can get everybody rounded up. I need people watching her momma, auntie and everybody else that this bitch might be in contact with. So, I can find my fucking baby who knows how long she plans on playing this game. I know that it is a nigga that got making these type of demands Quita every barely had fifty dollars; she has no idea what to do with 100,000. E and Gotti made their way outside.

"I called Dan at the dealership, I'm on my way up there now," E said handing me my phone back.

"Alright, call me if y'all hear anything," I said as I made my way to my car I have to get out here too.

Bad News, has sent word to get everybody that is affiliated to hit the streets. I'm not going to sleep until I have Hope. When I get my hands on that bitch I'm going to kill that bitch slow. I made my way over to where Quita's mom used to live. As I ride I can't help, but think what the fuck that bitch could be doing to my baby, she cut her fucking ponytail off. All the possibilities of what is could be going on is making me even fucking madder.

Quita playing the games with now she wants a car doesn't surprise me. That is the type of shit that she does. Her laughing about this shit and her already being able to imagine where my head is at is going to make her keep playing this game as long as she can. I pulled up on Peoria to the house that Cassie used to live in and it's white people going inside. I knew as I drove over here there is a chance that I she wouldn't live here anymore.

I have to go and check on Mina and talk to Brionna so I can see is if she can do something for me. I know that Mina is good with Brionna. Looking in my rearview mirror at Hope's car seat is fucking me up. People do all types of crazy shit to kids. If somebody does something to me I can handle it an defend myself my baby can't. I need Bad News in the streets right now. As I pulled up at Bad News's my phone is ringing and its Krack. I don't have time to talk t him right now I sent him to the voicemail.

Mina opened the door and fell into my arms still crying. I got her into the house and she is asking questions that I don't have the answer to. I can't tell Mina that; Mina is used to me being the one that handles everything. In her eyes I can solve everything and make everything okay. Not being able to is making me sick to my stomach. I finally got Mina to calm down and go lay down.

"Bri, I need to you to look up some people for me," I said.

"Alright, let me go and get my laptop," Brionna said, and disappeared.

Bri, can do all types of shit. She a professional at falsifying some shit. I got three id's that ain't in my name. I know that Bri can find up to date info on all of Quita's family probably hopefully Quita too. In minutes Bri, started to rattle off addresses for everybody I asked for. I should of did this shit from the beginning.

"Cassie Jones, is a resident at a nursing home," Brionna said.

Soon as visiting hours start I'll be there waiting for Quita. If she is here in Colorado I know that she'll be to see her momma bright and early. I'm getting impatient for E, to call me and let me know what is happening now with the damn car. We buy cars all the time and drive off and come back and do the paperwork later; I don't see what the fuck is taking so long.

"You know some nigga named O?" I asked.

Brionna knows a lot of muthafuckas in her business and if she knows this nigga then I think that he might be able to lead me to Quita. He starts popping up on the block and then Quita that can't be no fucking coincidence. I got everybody on the lookout for that nigga. He been on the block asking about me; so, he shouldn't be that hard to find. Brionna doesn't who the nigga is, but she grabbed her phone to call some people to see what she can find out. Shit, I don't know nothing about the nigga, so I can't even give a good fucking description on who he is.

My phone started ringing and it's Bad News. He confirmed they got O. I let Brionna know and made my way to talk to Mina before I leave. She's sleep; so, I just left her alone. I have to get to this bitch nigga and see where the fuck Quita is at. I made my way out to my car and made my way to the spot where they got this nigga at.

I jumped out Dirt and Gotti are standing by the door and I can hear Envii from way out here. What the fuck is she doing here? I thought her and E, weren't even speaking to each other. I'm not in the mood to deal with her load ass. When I walked into the spot, surprisingly Envii shut the fuck up. This nigga looks untouched like they just snatched him and brought him here and that is a problem for me.

"Lower him," I said as I walked to the middle of the floor where he is hanging at.

We haven't had to use this spot in a long time. I kept it just for emergencies like this one. They got this nigga hanging upside down, in chains his arms and legs both spread in different direction. I looked at Envii because I know she's the on that decided this was good way to restrain him.

"I did, I good muthafucking job I know. I'll give some kidnapping tips before we leave," Envii said.

I shook my head and turned back around to this nigga. O, is knocked out and I know Envii's dumb ass didn't think about him passing the fuck out from the blood rushing to his fucking head. She should have stayed her ass in school. I took out my lighter and started to burn his face with it and he woke right up.

As big as his eyes got he knows exactly who the fuck I am. "So, I hear been looking for me; what's up?" I said. He didn't say anything just started to choke uncontrollably looking around. O is laying flat on his back still in chains and on the concrete. I lost all the patience I had dealing with Quita earlier. That bitch got the car and I still don't have my daughter just like I knew she wasn't just going to give her up even after getting the car.

"Get him something to drink," I said as and Dirt went to get it.

"This that bitch now," E said walking out the warehouse.

Dirt came back handed me the can gas can filled with Gasoline. It 's filled to the top. I don't have all night and this nigga is about to start talking one way or another. I pushed my Glock into his mouth knocking out a few teeth in the process and opened up his mouth and proceeded to pour the gas down his throat. Enforcer came back into the room.

"This bitch making more requests K," E said.

I nodded my head and looked back at O and watched him, squirm and moving like he going to be able to bust out of these chains. Some muthafuckas is just dumb and even though is fucking extreme and I don't know why the fuck Envii did this shit I do know that fucking with her ass he ain't getting out of this shit on his on.

"Where is my daughter?" I asked.

"I don't know after she got the money; she left, and I haven't seen her since," O struggled to say.

I know her broke ass did she don't want to have to split the money with his ass or give him none of it. He ran down the motel they were staying at and Envii left out to go and look for her, but I know that bitch ain't staying there with that money that she got in her hands. He gave me the address to all the places that Bri had already gave me.

I started to pour the gas all over O and Dirt handed me a piece a paper and I lit it and threw I on him. I got to get to the nursing home to see momma Cassie.

# Gotti

"What do you want now Giordan?"

"Can you come by."

"You know I'm not. Gionni is at my house what the fuck would I need to come by your house for?"

Giordan is Gionni's mother and nothing else. Gionni is with me majority of the time. I haven't fucked with Giordan in years and the only reason why I talk to her now is because of Gionni. Giordan started to say something and I just hung up on her. Gionni is thirteen and I haven't fucked with Giordan since she was pregnant. You only get one time to play me and after that yo muthafuckin ass will not get another chance. The only reason why she still alive is because of Gionni.

As I pulled up at home I see Envii's car. Goddess is going to outpatient treatment trying to save face for her coworkers and these booshy muthafuckas neighbors. Damn shame I don't even want to go in my own house because of Envii loud ass. I can hear her loud ass from out here. I made my way in the house.

Goddess was coming down the stairs as I walked in the house.

"Hi, baby! How was your day?"

"It was alright, you good?"

I love my wife and I don't know what the fuck I would do without her. She understands me and is my peace from the streets. Goddess is beautiful smooth caramel skin, big pretty brown eyes and long straight black hair that is all hers. My wife is tall and thick in all the right places. Goddess is damn near perfect. She's smart, understanding and loyal.

We have good days and bad days just like everybody else, but the good outweighs the bad. I know why Goddess is with me and I know why I choose to be with her and at the time we both needed each other for various reasons. I still feel the same way about her that I did when we first got together.

"Your mom called," Goddess said.

"Alright, I'll call her."

As we made our way through the house my head started to pound. Envii was on the phone screaming at the top of her lungs. It is only so much of her ass that I can take. I don't see how the fuck Enforcer deals with that shit.

"Bitch, you just do yo muthafucking job! Did I hire you to be a muthafucking cheaters investigator? No bitch I didn't! Unless you would like to sit in the dark and not make it to Christmas I suggest you remember that!" Envii screamed into the phone and threw the phone across the room.

"You want to break shit I suggest you take yo ass home," I said, as Goddess was attempting to step in between Envii and me.

"Move Goddess."

"Genesis, let me deal with Envii."

"Fuck you! This is my sister's house too!"

"Envii, shut up or you can leave," Goddess said.

The only thing that stopped me from shooting Envii was Goddess and my nigga E and that's the only thing. I don't allow nobody to talk to me crazy if the bitch at Conoco get crazy it will be some niggas waiting for her to finish her shift. Envii is so disrespectful and she thinks she can talk to anybody any kind of way. I understand from being with Goddess that Envii and her have been through a lot. They mom wasn't shit and neither were their dads. Envii uses that shit as an excuse to act the way she does. The bitch needs to go to therapy. My phone started vibrating, I looked at it it's my dumb ass cousin Memphis.

"Dad, I don't have to go to my moms do I?" Gionni asked as she ran into the living room.

"No, you don't."

She handed me her phone with messages from Giordan saying she had to come home. I deleted all the messages and handed her back her phone. This is the type of shit that makes me want to fuck Giordan up.

"Is your homework done?"

"Yea."

Giordan is going to make me hurt her. Just when I thought I could come home and relax that's out the fucking question. I got up and grabbed my jacket Goddess met me at the door.

"Envii's leaving, Janice is on her way over," Goddess said.

"Good, I'll be right back. I gotta go handle something."

"Don't do anything to Giordan. Genesis."

I kissed Goddess and made my way out the door. Goddess and I don't discuss my business. She knows what I do and she knew what it was before we went on or first date but she wants no parts in that part of my life. Janice is Goddess's sponsor, so hopefully she is gone by the time I get back. She also knows the situation with Giordan. Giordan didn't give a fuck about me again until I got with Goddess. I made my way to Giordan's to make sure this bitch understands a few things.

I'm so damn mad as I got out of my truck that I left the door opened and didn't give a fuck. If any of these muthafuckas think about touching my truck they know what time it is. Giordan lives in the hood because she wants to pocket every dime she gets from me or anybody else. I pushed open Giordan's door, and it slammed into the wall. The picture that hung of her dead aunt Mable shattered and hit the floor. I don't give a fuck, I made my way up the stairs to find her.

"Giordan!" I screamed.

"Don't come in my house breaking shit. Take yo ass back to that bit..." Giordan attempted to say before I snatched her off her bed by her neck.

"Bitch, don't ever in yo life try to use my daughter to get to me. If you ever refer to my wife as anything other than her name bitch, you'll go missing."

Giordan was gasping for air; I didn't give a fuck. Giordan's damn near white skin in turning red. To a nigga in the streets you would look at Giordan and say she bad, but even though she pretty on the outside she's a ugly muthafucka on the inside. The bitch wanted me to come over so I'm here. As I looked at Giordan with her eyes bulging I thought about Gionni and dropped her to the floor.

"Gionni, won't be back here unless she decides she wants to see you. Don't call her, don't text her and if you show up at her school I will kill yo momma faster than she's already dying."

I made my out the house. Giordan is gasping for air. It didn't matter to me I needed to get to Memphis, dumb ass. Clearly today is get on my damn nerves day. As I made my way to Memphis my Kurupt's number flashed across the dashboard. With all the shit tht is going on right now I can only imagine what the fuck he is about to say.

"What's up K? I said as the call connected.

"Waiting for E, to get back and this fucking phone to ring. I need you to do something for me," K said.

"Say no more soon as I handle this other shit real fast I'm on my way," I said and we disconnected the call.

I called this bitch ass nigga Memphis back and he didn't answer. I called his ass again and he didn't answer. I have been waiting for this nigga to do his fucking job for days now. Family or not this nigga is getting to damn comfortable and today is the day his ass is going on notice.

"Muthafucka where you at so, we can get this shit over wit," I spit as the call connected.

"I'm in the middle of taking care of some—" Memphis attempted to say.

"I don't give a fuck if you were painting yo nails bitch! Where the fuck are you at?" I screamed into the phone.

"I'm at my baby mommas," Memphis said, breathing hard in my damn ear.

Memphis has one job to transport guns and nothing else. The only reason I have him doing that is because he's getting them from his brother. I'll figure something else out because this isn't working.

"I was just trying to tell you that I'm ready."

"Nigga you ready for what? You got one job and if that ain't working for you I suggest you figure something else out."

All these calls and texts in between is fucking unnecessary. I don't have time to sit on the phone with no damn body. Memphis been blowing up my phone trying to meet up, but then he can only do it at specific time. This nigga is jump slow; I'm convinced that he should be getting a fucking check.

"I know but I can do more..."

"Look muthafucka after this next time coming up. I'm done with yo ass. Do not fucking leave that house until I get there or your dead."

I don't have patience and clearly, he thinks because we're cousins he gets some special pass but he doesn't. I'm not giving my momma pass or nobody else's momma a pass. I don't know why muthafuckas insist on playing with me today. Momma flashed across the dashboard.

"Yes, momma," I said.

"Genesis, come by we need to talk," my mother Nancy said.

"Alright I'm on my way," I said and disconnected the call.

I know why she is calling me and it's not because she fucking wants to talk. We talk enough. It ain't shit that she could possibly want to talk to me about. I made my way over to my momma's so I can get this shit over with and get to Memphis. I pulled up to my momma's and jumped out. I wish she would leave this house, but he refuses to. I see my sister Modesty's car in the driveway and she is supposed to be at school. The school I'm paying all this fucking money for her to go to for her black ass not to be there. I let myself in and Modesty damn jumped off the couch when she saw me.

"Why the fuck are you not at school?" I asked.

"I needed a break," Modesty said shrugging her shoulders.

"I'm going to break yo fucking face. If you don't get the fuck out of here and go to school," I said walking up on Modesty.

Modesty is eighteen and she lives with Goddess and I. The only time she comes over here is when she on some good bullshit because she knows that she can get away with that shit over here. It's not about the money, but I want Modesty to something with her life and get the fuck out of here. She's not going to do that from over here sitting on the couch with momma. Modesty hugged and kissed my mom and made her way to the door.

"Either you go to school or I'm taking my fucking car and yo ass will be on the bus!" I screamed, before the front door closed behind Modesty.

I handed my momma what the fuck she wanted and the reason why she was calling me. You can say the fuck you want to say about me; if she doesn't get it from me then she's going to get it from the nigga around the corner! It's not about the money I can't buy toilet paper to fill the bathrooms in my house for a month with the money I get from my mom. I don't want my mom out on here getting shit from any of these niggas out here. My mom has been on drugs for years ever since my dad left her. I can't make her get help and she doesn't want help and I accepted that a long time ago.

Before then we had a damn near perfect family. My mother was teaching school at Smith and my father was preacher. I met Enforcer at church; are dads were good friends. One night my mom picked up the phone and heard my dad on the phone with some deacon from the church talking about how he wanted to suck his dick. My mom confronted him while he was on the phone and they got into an argument he left, and I haven't seen him since that night.

Ever since that night my mom has never been the same. We never talked about it; we just acted like it never happened. My mom hasn't stepped foot in a church since that happened and neither have I. That's why when Goddess and I got married I wouldn't get married in a church. Mina was so young I don't even think that she would remember it happened.

"How is Goddess doing?" My mother asked.

"She's alright. I have to go we still looking for Hope," I said as I kissed my mom on the check and picked up my money off the coffee table and made my way out the door.

# Kai Morae

---

*I*'m trying to focus and keep my eyes open. This is the worst headache that I ever had in my life. I'm looing around the room trying to weigh my options on what the fuck I am going to do to get out of here. I can hear Memphis is the other room talking, but I don't hear Deontae.

I don't have any time to waste and laying on this floor crying and thinking about and blaming myself for all the fucked-up decisions that I made isn't going to get me anywhere. I'm struggling to get off the floor and not lose my balance and smack onto the floor. I started to bang on the bedroom door; while praying that Deontae isn't here right now. I'm not sure what time it is, but now it's dark outside.

I can hear somebody, putting a key in the door so, I stopped knocking. I backed up from the door so, whoever it is can get in. Luckily it is Memphis and he's dumber that Deontae, so I can play his ass easier.

"You want some water?" Memphis said, handing me a bottle of water.

"Thank you," I said taking the water and taking it to the head.

Memphis phone started ringing and whoever it is mad as fuck

and calling him all types punk bitches. I know that if Deontae was here he would have been in here getting Memphis the fuck out of my face. So, he must be gone somewhere.

"Can you hand me my purse, so that I can get a Tylenol out of it," I said.

Memphis jumped up and went and got my bag. I finished off the bottle of water and I'm still thirsty. Memphis came back still on the phone and handed me my bag. I found what the fuck I needed and it's not a damn Tylenol. I pulled out Sean's gun and put it to Memphis's head. His eyes got as big as golf balls and he dropped his phone to the ground. When the phone smacked the ground, a nigga said that he was outside. I shot Memphis in his head and he slapped the tiled floor causing a loud thump to echo throughout the room.

I've been around guns most of my life, but actually pulling a trigger was something that I never thought that I would have to do. I can't stop looking at Memphis lifeless body laying in front of me. His eyes are wide open and even though, I know he is dead and isn't breathing it's like he is looking straight at me.

"Kai," I heard a man's voice say.

I looked up pointing the gun in the man's direction and it's Gotti. He tried to grab the gun out of my hand, but I still have a tight grip on it. Gotti was able to snatch the gun from my hand. I don't know why he is her, but I have never been so damn happy to see him in my life.

"Kai, come out you got to get out of here. Go to my truck and and I'll be right out," Gotti said putting his truck keys in my hand.

I snapped out of the daze I was in and snatched up my purse from the ground and the fuck out of the house. With each step I take it feels like pens and needles are sticking me. My entire body is in pain, but right now none of that shit matters. Even though Gotti and I never had a close relationship they way that K always talked about him I know that he is a real one and will handle everything.

"Pop the trunk," Gotti hollered from outside the truck.

I popped the trunk and Gotti put two oversized duffle bags in the trunk and went back and did a light jog back to the house. I went thorough my purse looking for a Tylenol to take until I can get to something stronger. Gotti came back to the trunk with two more duffle bags slammed the trunk and got in.

As we drove I don't know what the fuck to say to Gotti. How do I explain what happened back there when I know he knows how things ended between Kamal and me because of what the fuck I chose to do. I'm ashamed that I put myself in a position for that shit to happen to me.

"Thank you Gotti," I finally said.

"You good," Gotti said and kept bobbing his head to the Jeezy that is coming out of his speakers.

Now that I am out of there I have to figure out what the fuck am I going to do. Deontae emptied out my bank account. And I'm sure found my stash at the house and took that too. With him still being alive I can't go back to my apartment. I'm damn sure not going back to my aunt Lisa's. We pulled up to Gotti and Goddess home. I looked at the time before I got out the truck and it's damn near three in the morning.

"You can stay here for the night," Gotti said as he led the way into their palace.

Their house is beautiful it reminds me a lot of K's place. I've only been over here once and it looks like they have made a lot of changes since then. I feel like a fucking bum and I know that I look like one too. The fact that I know that Gotti is going to tell Kamal that he seen me and my current position is what embarrasses me the most. Goddess is running down the left side of their double staircase as I walked in the house.

Gotti disappeared and Goddess was being her normal self. She is willing to help anybody and by doing all that she can. She led the way to one of their nine bedrooms. She keeps offering me food and something to drink. Goddess is a truly good persona and has a heart made of gold with no malice or ill intentions. By the concern in her face as she looked over my body, the scars, bruises and the overall condition that I am in I know that she has questions, but she hasn't asked them.

"Goddess, I am fine. I appreciate you and Gotti letting me stay here," I said.

"You already know that I will help you any way that I can and Gotti must think your okay otherwise he would have left you where he found you at," Goddess said laughing.

Goddess has clothes and pajamas with the tags laid out on the bed. I'm guessing that they must be Modesty's because they damn sure ain't Goddesses size. Goddess showed me where everything that I would need is at to be able to get myself together and somebody started knocking on the door. I turned to see who it was and it's Gotti.

"Here this should help with some of the pain. If you don't feel better in the morning Goddess will call her people to come see about you," Gotti said handing me two pills and leaving back out the room.

"I'm going to call my friend Dr. Maci, I think you need someone to check you out just in case," Goddess said.

All I want to do is get in the hot steaming shower and go to sleep. I know that it is going to hurt like hell, but right now that is all I want. I will deal with everything else when I wake up. I need to call Katrina back who has called me so many damn times, but I'll do that in the morning because that is probably where I'm going to be living.

"If you need anything, we are at the very end of the hallway," Goddess said.

"I'll be fine. You have done more than enough," I said.

I don't know what all Gotti has told Goddess about what happened earlier. I also don't know what she knows about K and me. I am going to get some rest and come up with a plan. Gotti is always very short with everybody. I have never heard him say too much so he is hard to read. If he didn't really want me here I would never know unless he said it. I know that I can't live here so I have to what the fuck I know how to do and make a way out of no way.

~

As I opened my eyes, it's still dark outside. I feel like I have been sleeping forever. I grabbed my phone off the night stand and I have.

It's nine o clock at night. I have to get up and get out of here. I slipped off the clothes that Goddess gave me and called Katrina; her ass is going to have to come and get me.

"Bitch, where have you been?" Katrina screamed in the phone.

"I'll tell you in a minute, I need you to come and get me," I said as Goddess knocked on the door of the bedroom.

"Your up, how are you feeling?" Goddess asked.

I told Katrina I would text her the address and got off the phone with her. If staying at her house dealing with her and her nigga for the week shit don't make me get my shit together fast then nothing will.

"I'm feeling better; I'm going to go on head and go," I said, looking through my purse.

"You do not have to go Kai. You can stay here as long s you need to," Goddess said.

"Kai, get yo shit and come on," I heard a man say.

I looked up at the door and it's Kamal. The look in his eyes I have never seen before. Goddess knows something because she snatched my charger out the wall and handed me some shoes. Kamal left from the doorway and I can hear him and Gotti talking. Goddess told me to call her and was helping me off the bed like I'm cripple. I can't say that I am not happy to see K but knowing that Deontae is still out here I don't want to bring any of that to him.

Goddess told me to call her and we made our way out of the room. K and Gotti are standing at the bottom of the stair case. The hate that is in K's eyes is making me uncomfortable and uneasy. I know that I deserve it all for how I played the situation and the situation that I am in now all I can hope is that he will hear me out.

As Goddess walked me out to K's truck he opened the door and got in the driver side slamming the door making the windows shake. I got in the truck and Tupac "When We Ride On Our Enemies" started to blast through the speakers as K started up the truck and sped off. K hasn't looked at me or said one word every time his phone rings he looks at it and keeps ignoring the calls. I can't say anything about him being cold and not being the loving man that he was when I first met him. As he turned the corner I grabbed the arm rest, his arm was resting on and he snatched his arm away. Tears started to form in my eyes and before I knew it they are falling down my face faster than I can wipe them.

K pulled up to a home that is a few blocks away from Gotti's. He slammed the car in park and grabbed his phone and called somebody said, "Hold em," and hung up. K turned down the music that is making my headache worse than it already is. I checked my phone and Katrina is calling me. I sent her to voicemail, I'll call her back in a minute.

"Kamal, I'm sorr—" I attempted to say before he threw up his hand which caused me to jump.

"You think I'm gone hit you? You been fucking with that bitch nigga too long. I don't want to hear that shit so save it," Kamal said, reaching over me and opening the glove compartment taking out an envelope.

A black Audi, pulled up into the circular driveway facing us. The nigga in the car nodded his head. I want to apologize for everything that I have done. I know I was wrong and I knew it shortly after I did it. It didn't take for me to go through that shit last night to know that Deontae wasn't shit. He showed me his true colors a long time ago.

"Stay here; go to work, school and come back here. You can drive the Lexus truck in the garage. If you need anything Ace or Big Face will make sure that you get it," K said putting the envelope in my lap.

A nigga opened the truck door and I looked at Kamal and he switched the truck into drive and wouldn't look at me still. I got out the truck and made my way into the house. I looked back hoping that Kamal was coming in, but he sped out of the driveway only causing me to cry harder than I was. I looked out the window and the nigga that pulled up in the Audi is still sitting out there. I pulled out my phone and Gina has called me three times. I dialed 611 to change my phone number right now.

I hear a phone ringing, so I made my way through the house to find it. I'm still waiting for slow ass T Mobile, to answer the fucking phone. This house is amazing but being in this big ass house alone is making me feel more alone than I already am inside. The phone stopped ringing as I came up on a big ass living room with fish tanks covering one of the long ass walls. The phone started ringing again and I see it across the room on an end table. I struggle to get over to it; I am still fucked up. I picked up the phone and nobody isn't saying anything.

"When I call this phone you need to answer," K said.

"Okay."

"Nobody needs to know where the fuck you at, but me," K said and disconnected the call.

An operator at T Mobile finally came on the line and I told her to change my number and she put me on hold. I don't give a fuck today how long I need to hold this number is getting changed today. Katrina is blowing up my phone, but she is going to have to wait. I made my way up stairs and walked room to room taking all of this in. every room is fully furnished with bed room suits and tv's n the walls. I made it all the way down the hall to the last room and opened the door. This has to be the master bedroom because it is the biggest room.

It is a California king bed, with a cushioned headboard. Curtains hanging from the ceiling on the sides of the bed are pulled back to the wall. I made my way to the closet and it is filled with clothes. They are color coordinated in each section of the closet. The shoe racks are filled with tennis shoes and heels of every kind that you could want. I spotted a chase chair that matches the décor and laid down on it. The fucking lady at T Mobile finally did what-ever she needed to do and got my number changed.

As I lay here I can't help, but to think about what I am going to do. Yes, K has put this together for me, but I need to be able to handle shit on my own. I can't stay here forever. He won't even look at me and doesn't want to hear shit that I have to say. I picked up my phone; I need to call Katrina back. Her ass didn't answer, but text me saying she is on the phone with Enforcer. I thought I was fucking dumb bitches ain't shooting up my house for no nigga.

The door bell is ringing so, I got up to see who it is. It's probably the nigga that K has watching me. I made my way down stairs and it's Goddess so, I opened the door. She is always so happy and in good spirits. I'm just happy that somebody is here if only for a little while.

"I brought some food over for you, so won't have to worry about cooking tonight," Goddess said as she led the way through the house.

"Thanks, you didn't have to do that."

I know that everybody isn't out to get you and there are some good people left in the world, but they are far and in between in my life. As I jumped up on a barstool in the kitchen rang again and Goddess made her way out to go and get it. I'm glad she bought some food because I'm fucking starving.

"Why the fuck did he move her to this house instead of just of just moving her to the house and why is Ace bitch ass sitting outside?" Envii asked loud as hell; they all the way down the hall I can still hear her.

"Envii, shut up damn. I don't know," Goddess said.

"Damn," Envii said as she walked in the room taking in how fucked up I am.

Goddess hit Envii and Envii made her way around sit next to me. Goddess is one thing, but Envii is a whole another breed of female and hearing her opinion about the shit I've done I know is going to be way different than what Goddess is going to have to say. Goddess is putting a salad together and it's just awkward and too damn quiet for me.

"I'm not like Goddess. I'm not about to come over here cook for you bitch I don't' cook for myself. What the fuck happened and start from the beginning why the fuck did you leave K," Envii said breaking the awkward silence.

Goddess stopped what she was doing to turn around and face me. I started from the beginning telling them about Millie and Envii cut me right the fuck off, but Goddess shut her up, so I got back to telling them everything. The way Envii is looking at me I don't know she wants to fight or to just cut my ass off again. Goddess is just shaking her head looking at me with so much sympathy. I told them everything that happened at the house with

Memphis; shit that was it. They know what happened with K, shit I'm here.

"I'm just going to be honest with you, but your fucking dumb," Envii said and then taking a drink of juice.

"I'll take that. I fucked up," I said.

"So, what the fuck did K say to you?" Envii asked.

"Nothing," I said.

"Both of y'all are dumb and y'all belong together. I wouldn't have bitch in my house and not address our fucking issues. I would have called you all types of stupid, dumb bitches beat yo ass and then depending how bad I fucked you up maybe I'd let you stay," Envii said and then walked out of the room to take a call.

"Please excuse my sister. She doesn't know how to talk to people. K, has a lot going on with Hope missing. Right now, nothing matters until Hope gets home," Goddess said, as she went back to getting the food ready.

"Missing? What is going on?" I asked.

Goddess started to tell me everything that is going on. Hope has been missing for two days. They paid the first ransom and now they have a second one and Hope still is not home. I feel even worse than I already felt. I'm sitting here feeling sorry for myself for some shit that I got myself in and Hope fucking missing. I know how much K loves and cares about Hope, so I can't even imagine what he is going through.

"So, I have to go run and get this bitch out of the closet," Envii said as she came back into the closet.

"Out of a closet?" Goddess asked.

"Yes, bitch I know that device is working in your ear; out of a closet. She should have been doing her fucking job and she wouldn't have had to be in the damn closet," Envii said.

I have seen Envii in action and I know after what she did at Katrina's. Putting a bitch in a closet is nothing compared to what the fuck else she will do. Goddess and Envii are later water and oil and all they do is argue whenever I have ever been around them. I can't believe they even talk to each other.

"Come ride with me so we can finish talking," Envii said.

"I can't," I said.

"You physically can't walk. I thought that you just got beat up a little bit," Envii said moving her hands.

"No, K doesn't want me to leave the house," I said.

"So, he bought you here to be house a slave. Goddess while, I'm gone tell this bitch when slavery ended," Envii said and made her way out the house.

My phone started going off alerting me that I have a message on messenger. I looked and it's a message from my cousin Reign saying that my cousin Dink got shot.

CPSIA information can be obtained
at www.ICGtesting.com
Printed in the USA
LVHW01s0001250718
584785LV00025B/410/P